ELMER KELTON

DONOVAN

FORGE®

A TOM DOHERTY ASSOCIATES BOOK
NEW YORK

This is a work of fiction. All the characters and events portrayed in this book are either products of the author's imagination or are used fictitiously.

DONOVAN

Copyright © 1961, 1986 by Elmer Kelton

A Forge Book
Published by Tom Doherty Associates, LLC
175 Fifth Avenue
New York, NY 10010

www.tor.com

Forge® is a registered trademark of Tom Doherty Associates, LLC.

ISBN: 0-765-34300-2

First Forge edition: November 2003

Printed in the United States of America

0 9 8 7 6 5 4 3 2 1

Praise for Elmer Kelton

"Recently voted 'the greatest Western writer of all time' by the Western Writers of America, Kelton creates characters more complex than L'Amour's. . . . Kelton adds surprisingly strong elements of humanity, remorse, reversals of character, and terrific nobility for 'the red devils'. Wonderfully satisfying, sophisticated, unsentimental, superbly crafted, and full of a whopping good humor out of Twain. Hard to beat."
—*Kirkus Reviews*

"A solid story of murder, revenge and Indian fighting, in which almost everyone but the unlikely hero is quick on the draw. . . . This is a rousing tale of the Texas Rangers, early Texas history and of a brave and thoughtful young Westerner."
—*Publishers Weekly* on *The Buckskin Line*

"Kelton spins a good yarn. The settings are true to Texas. It is, however, his characterizations that move him from being a writer of "Westerns" to recognition as one of America's foremost writers . . . *Cloudy in the West* lends itself to comparison with *Huckleberry Finn*."
—*Review of Texas Books*

"Kelton, like fine wine, just keeps getting better and better."
—*Tulsa World*

"Elmer Kelton again proves he's one of America's premiere storytellers."
—*True West* on *The Way of the Coyote*

"Elmer Kelton is one of America's great storytellers. His work gives me a complete sense of that Texas fiber that carries from the frontier to modern times. His characters, native and settlers alike, bounce with resilience and determination. It would be difficult to find a more engaging writer than Elmer Kelton."
—Earl Murray

"[Kelton takes] meticulous care with setting, landscape and historical authenticity. . . . [This is] ambrosia for lovers of Western novels."
—*Fort Worth Morning Star-Telegram* on *Ranger's Trail*

Other Books by Elmer Kelton

1

EVEN BEFORE HIS HORSE'S EARS SUDDENLY POINTED FOR-
ward, Webb Matlock was becoming uneasy. He had
slipped his saddlegun out of its scabbard beneath his leg and
had lifted it up across the pommel, on the ready. He pulled
the dun horse to a halt and raised his left hand as a signal
to the riders with him.

"Easy, boys. We don't want to be in no hurry about this
thing."

Webb Matlock wore a sheriff's badge. With him rode five
men from the Box L cow outfit, hurriedly deputized to help
him run out the trail of some would-be cattle thieves. Johnny
Willet and another Box L hand had come unexpectedly upon
a half a dozen men hazing 70 or 80 of Old Man Jess Leggett's good cows south toward the Rio Grande. Rather than
tackle the rustlers themselves, they had pulled back unseen
and spurred to the ranch headquarters.

For several years now, Old Man Jess had been bringing
in good Durham bulls to breed out the Longhorn strain. He
was proud of these halfbreed cows and didn't want to lose
any of them. Over and above that, he held a deep and abiding
hatred for thieves. In olden times, before there had been law
to look to, he had shot or hanged them himself. This time
he had sent for Webb Matlock. Then, instead of waiting, the
impatient old man had taken his cowboys and set out in

pursuit. They fought a running battle that forced the thieves to give up the cattle. But Old Jess had fallen with a bullet in his shoulder. That had stopped the pursuit until Webb got there.

The last thing Jess had hollered at Webb as they had hauled him toward town in a wagon was: "You get 'em now, you hear?"

This was the Texas border country, and *ladrones* out of Mexico sometimes still came over the border to hit and run, steal and carry off whatever they could get away with. In many people on both sides of the river, old hatreds still burned. To some on the south side, the Texas revolution and the Mexican war had meant nothing. To these this land still rightfully belonged to Mexico, and so did everything that walked upon it.

Webb had asked Johnny Willet, "Mexicans, Johnny?"

Johnny had been riding in a strange, thoughtful silence. He shook his head. "Mostly it was *gringos*. Odd thing about one of them, he . . ." Johnny broke off. "Forget it, you wouldn't believe it."

"Believe what, Johnny?"

"Nothin', it was a crazy notion." He changed the subject. "I'm pretty sure we hit one of them. He slumped over, nearly fell off his horse. Got away into the brush, though, and that was the last we seen of him."

A mile or so back they had come upon a blood-crusted handkerchief lying amid the fresh horsetracks, and they had known for sure.

Now Webb sat rigid in the saddle, squinting into a brushy header where in rainy times the water would come rushing off the sides of the rocky hills to spread out down a silty mesquite draw. Webb Matlock was a medium-tall man in his early thirties, a little on the stocky side but without any fat on him. He had a square face, a strong jaw that showed the dark stubble of two days' whiskers. His gray eyes were habitually squinted a little, for this was a land of harsh sunlight, dust, and wind. He was a sober, serious man for the most part, so much so that people who didn't know sometimes guessed him to be much older than he was. He had toted his own load since before he was fifteen.

The black-tipped ears of his dun horse were still pointed forward. Looking around him, Matlock could see that a couple of the other horses were the same.

Something ahead of us yonder, he thought. *Pity a man can't be as smart as a horse.*

He made a sweeping motion with his hand. "Fan out, boys. Couple of you work up the hill on one side of that header, a couple on the other. Better go afoot. Ollie Reed, what say you hold the horses."

Ollie Reed, 50 now and bald as an egg, was glad enough to accept that chore. He was not the contentious kind.

Halfway out of his saddle, Johnny Willet stopped himself and asked, "Webb, what *you* aimin' to do?"

"You don't flush quail by ridin' around them. Somebody's got to go on in."

The sheriff swung to the ground to make himself less of a target. He stood behind his horse for cover and peered across the saddle, looking for signs of anything in the brush. He waited then, giving the men time to work up the hills on either side of the header. Once they were there, they should have a good view of whatever might be below them. They could provide cover for Webb when he moved in.

Ollie Reed's voice was thin with excitement. "I don't like this, Webb, don't like it atall. Puts me in mind of the days when Clabe Donovan and his bunch was runnin' loose."

"Clabe Donovan's dead, Ollie."

Ollie nodded, shivering "That don't keep me from rememberin'."

Not many years ago, Clabe Donovan and a wild bunch that ran with him were cutting a wide swath through the border country, jumping back and forth across the Rio Grande, stealing what they wanted, killing when someone got in their way. Donovan caught the blame for just about everything bad that happened in those days. Likely it wasn't all justified, but he had gloried in it anyway, perversely proud that he was becoming a legend while he still lived.

In death, the legend had kept on growing.

Webb's horse nickered. An answering nicker came from within the thorny tangle of mesquite. Limbs crackled. A riderless bay horse broke into the open, moving in a long trot. He came straight toward the possemen's horses and stopped among them.

Webb saw blood splotches on the saddle.

He glanced at the wide-eyed Ollie Reed. "There's probably a rustler lyin' in yonder dead."

"And again, maybe he ain't," Reed observed nervously. "Wounded animal is the most dangerous kind."

"A man's different from an animal."

"Some of them ain't."

Webb handed Ollie his bridle reins. "We'll find out pretty quick." Holding the saddlegun ready, he started toward the brush afoot. He moved cautiously from one mesquite to another, keeping himself behind cover of the green leaves as much as he could. A cold tingle ran up and down his back. His sweaty shirt clung to him.

A bullet whined by his head. Leaves drifted down from a mesquite where the slug had clipped them. He threw himself to the ground, breaking his fall first with his knees, then with the butt of the rifle. He snapped a shot in the direction from which the report had come. A second bullet buzzed angrily overhead.

Six-shooter. Webb could tell by the sound. Six-shooter must be all the man had. If he had a rifle he would have used it. At this range, only the rankest kind of luck would score the man a hit. The sheriff levered another cartridge into the breech, pushed to his knees, and sprinted again. This time he saw the flash. The saddlegun was nearly torn from his hands. Splinters drove searing hot into his skin. The bullet had glanced off the wooden stock.

He saw a depression ahead, with a bush beyond to help hide him. He dived, sliding in the loose rocks, ripping his clothing, tearing his flesh. He knew he was bruised blue. Breathing hard, he paused to wipe sweat from his forehead onto his sleeve. He listened, hearing movement as the gunman tried to shift position. Webb called:

"This is Sheriff Matlock. We got you surrounded. No

sense in you fightin' anymore. Throw your gun out and raise up where we can see you."

Another shot sent more mesquite leaves showering down.

Webb called again: "You're playin' the fool. If you're wounded, you need doctorin'. Don't just lay there and die."

He heard a cough. A weak voice said, "You'd never get me to town. You'd hang me."

"Nobody'll molest you, I give my word on that."

Johnny Willet was cautiously working his way back down the hillside. The cowboy paused tensely and caught the sheriff's eye. He held up one finger. Just one man, that was all.

The sheriff tried reasoning again. "You haven't got a chance, so why keep on with it? Don't make us have to kill you." He held his breath, waiting for an answer that didn't come. "There's already been enough blood spilled. We don't want any more."

Johnny Willet was moving in closer.

"Last chance," Webb called. "What do you say?"

The outlaw squeezed off another shot. It kicked dirt into Webb Matlock's eyes. The sheriff blinked desperately to clear away the burning, the momentary blindness.

He could hear Johnny's voice. "All right now, mister, how about it?"

Webb heard a desperate cry as the outlaw flopped over to see the man who had crept up on him unseen. The pistol cracked. Then Willet's rifle roared. Webb heard a groan. The pistol fell, rattling upon the rocks.

Webb stood up rubbing his eyes, blinking away the sand. He could see the cowboys closing in. Johnny Willet stood slump-shouldered, the smoking rifle held slackly in one hand. He glanced up as the sheriff reached him.

"Sometimes, Johnny, a man's got no choice. Did he hit you?"

Eyes bleak, Johnny shook his head. "Missed. Scared, I reckon. Took a wild shot."

"Next one might not've been so wild. You had to shoot him."

Willet's mouth twisted. "That don't make it no easier." He walked off into the brush to stand alone, his back turned.

The gunman lay twisted, face to the ground, legs drawn up in dying agony. Breath still struggled in him, but it wouldn't last long. Gently Webb turned him over. His heart went sick.

Gray-haired Uncle Joe Vickers, the Box L foreman, took a long look and cursed softly. "A button, Webb, not a day over twenty! Just a slick-faced kid is all!"

Webb knelt beside the dying youth. "Can you hear me, boy?"

The youngster tried hard. He managed a weak "Yes."

"They just threw you away, kid. They left you to cover for them, and they ran off. Who was it?"

The boy didn't answer.

Webb said, "You don't owe them a thing now, son. Tell us, who was it?"

His lips painfully attempted to form the word. "Dono . . . Donovan."

Webb looked quickly up at the perplexed faces around him. He said, "Boy, that can't be. Donovan is dead."

The youngster started again. "Don . . . Don . . ." The voice trailed off and he was gone.

Webb stayed on one knee. Despite the heat, a chill played up and down his back. Presently he said, "That's the strangest thing I ever heard. Everybody knows Donovan is dead."

Uncle Joe Vickers' face had turned as gray as ashes. "Sure we know. It was me that killed him!"

Webb Matlock closed his eyes, remembering the violent night Clabe Donovan's wild border-jumping career had suddenly been brought to a close. Donovan had had a brother named Morg, a salty young hellion a few years younger than himself. Morg had been a reckless rider, a good shot, a headstrong desperado of Clabe's own stripe. One thing he had lacked had been Clabe's shrewd judgment. Trying to pull a robbery on his own, Morg had gotten himself into a jackpot he couldn't get out of alone. Clabe had come to his rescue. Morg had escaped, but Clabe's horse had been hit. Left afoot, Clabe was tracked down like a wild animal.

His trial had been short, the verdict certain. And the sentence: to hang by the neck until dead.

Morg had made a big effort one night to free his brother. He had sent part of the Donovan bunch to one end of Dry Fork to set up a diversion and draw much of the guard away from the jail. Then he had moved in with the rest of the men. They stormed the jail and broke Clabe out. But spurring away, they rode into a deadly barrage of bullets.

Clabe Donovan's trademark had always been a black Mexican hat with peaked crown and wide brim. Uncle Joe Vickers had seen that hat and had stepped out into the dusty, dark street with a double-barreled shotgun. He had triggered both barrels at once. His target had rolled in the dirt, face blasted away. He had been dead before he hit the ground.

The people of Dry Fork never doubted the man's identity. They buried him and put up a marker: *Clabe Donovan.* The Donovan gang disappeared. Some said Morg had tried later to rob a mint deep down in Mexico and had been cut down by the *rurales*. Nobody worried much about Morg. Main thing was that Clabe was dead, and this section of the border country had comparative peace for the first time in years.

Sure, there were stories, persistent stories that came from God knows where, rumors that Clabe Donovan still lived down in Mexico. Those kinds of stories arose about every well-known outlaw. Always, after a passage of time, there were some who claimed the man had never really died. There were those who claimed to have seen him alive, long after the man had been buried.

At Dry Fork, men shrugged off such stories. They knew, for Uncle Joe Vickers had killed Clabe Donovan, and nearly everybody in Dry Fork had gone down to the cemetery to watch the outlaw's wooden coffin lowered into the grave. In time, souvenir hunters had whittled away so much of the simple little cross that the county had had to put up a new one.

Donovan, the young rustler had said. *Donovan!*

Johnny Willet had heard. Slowly he came back and stood looking down at this youngster he had killed. Voice unsteady, he said, "Webb, that's what I started to tell you while ago, only the more I thought about it, the crazier it seemed. I remember seein' Clabe Donovan in his prime. I'll never forget the way he looked, tall, straight, broad-shouldered, with that big black Mexican hat."

He looked around at the other men and said shakily, "I got in pretty close to them cow thieves today. If I hadn't known better, I'd have sworn one of them was Clabe Donovan, black hat and all!"

No effort was made to go on with the chase. In the first place, no one had the spirit for it now. In the second, tracks showed the rustlers had been gone a long time. They had simply left the wounded boy to die because they knew he would anyway, and he would slow them down. They probably had hoped for him to delay pursuit. That he had done.

"Not much use goin' any farther," Webb said. "They'll be across the river before we can catch them anyhow."

Beyond the river lay the wild and brushy sanctuary that was Mexico. There the *gringo* lawman was never welcome. Decades of border warfare had left in much of the Mexican population a mortal hatred for the *rinches*, a term they applied to Rangers and all other *gringo* officers. There the *gringo* lawbreaker could find safety, even a welcome of sorts, so long as he spent good money and did not unduly disturb the people.

Webb Matlock looked down at the body. "It'd take us till this time tomorrow to get him to town. We better not wait that long."

Uncle Joe Vickers said, "There's a Box L line shack back yonderway. I expect we could find a shovel."

All they found for identification was a letter, carried in the shirt pocket so long that the envelope was beginning to wear through at the edges. They rolled the body in a slicker and tied it across the bay horse the young outlaw had been riding. At the line shack they found a shovel but no Bible. They dug a grave, and Webb Matlock stood over it with bared head, repeating the Twenty-third Psalm by heart.

Afterwards, the grave covered and a mound tamped over it, the gray-haired foreman said, "We'll put up some sort of a marker. Ordinarily I'd be inclined to leave a cow thief lay where he fell. But this one bein' just a kid and all . . ."

Webb nodded. "It's a long way to town, Uncle Joe. I expect I'd best be gettin' started."

"We'll go with you," said Vickers, "me and Ollie Reed. We're anxious to see how Jess Leggett's gettin' along. That old man's a way too ancient to be carryin' a slug in his shoulder . . ."

For the first time, Webb had to suppress a smile. The worried foreman lacked only three or four years being as old as his boss.

Camped on the trail that night, Webb kept remembering. The dying outlaw's words came back to him again and again. *Donovan. Donovan.*

"Uncle Joe," he said, "is there a chance you could've been mistaken? Is there a chance the man you shot *wasn't* Clabe Donovan?"

Fiercely Joe Vickers responded, "No sir, there ain't. I seen him!"

But the old man stared into the firelight, doubt coming into his eyes.

And Ollie Reed murmured wonderingly to himself, "Clabe Donovan, come back to life. Now, ain't that somethin'?"

2

DRY FORK WAS AN UNPLANNED, UNPRETTY SCATTERING OF lumber and adobe houses, most of them better called shacks. A rock courthouse and a few solid-looking business buildings put up in the last few years revealed a hope that better times waited somewhere ahead. At the south end, by coincidence on the side that lay nearest Mexico, was the town's sizeable Mexican settlement. It looked even poorer than the unassuming Anglo side.

Tired and much-sweated in the afternoon sun, three riders stirred a flurry of interest as they rode their flagging horses down the wagon-rutted, hoof-scarred street. It was not the men themselves so much as the riderless horse they led, a gunbelt hanging from the horn of an empty saddle. They stopped first at the doctor's house near the head of the street. Webb tarried only long enough to reassure himself that Jess Leggett was going to make out all right. In fact, Jess was already raising cain because two of his men had come to see about him. One, he maintained, would have been plenty.

"I ought to dock your wages," he told Ollie Reed, "because you sure can't claim you're workin'."

Old Jess didn't mean it, for attention really pleased him. That he felt like hell-raising was a good sign. He never spoke kindly except when he was sick.

Webb swung back into the saddle and moved on down the

street toward Quince Pyburn's livery stable. At the little Dry Fork cafe, Ellie Donovan stepped out onto the small shaded porch to watch silently as Webb rode by. Webb raised his hand, and she nodded to him, a fleeting smile crossing her face. Her gaze fell upon the led horse, and it stayed there.

What am I going to tell Ellie? Webb asked himself darkly. *What can I say?*

Quince Pyburn stood in the stable's big open door. He was a tall, gaunt man with a slight stoop to his shoulders, the look of hard years in his squinted eyes. He watched Webb Matlock ride in and dismount. The liveryman's gaze drifted over the led horse, but he was a patient man, not given to probing questions. He knew Webb would tell him when he was ready.

The sheriff said, "I got a saddle here to sell, Quince. You interested?"

Pyburn shrugged. "Man can always use an extra saddle around a barn like this. The gun too?"

Webb nodded. "It won't be of no use to *him* anymore. The money might be of some use to his mother."

Pyburn's eyebrows lifted. "Mother?" He looked at the horse again, frowning. "Forty dollars for the saddle and gun." That was overgenerous. "How about the horse?"

Matt shook his head. "Got a Rafter T brand on his hip. I'll take him home tomorrow." His mouth was set grimly as he wondered how the young rustler came to be riding a Rafter T horse in the first place.

Quince said, "I guess Bronc Tomlin will have some explainin' to do."

"He'll just say the horse was stolen. I couldn't prove different. But I'm goin' to talk with him anyhow. Might throw a scare into him."

Webb unsaddled his dun horse and turned him loose in a corral behind the barn. He left his saddle, blanket and bridle on a rack that had long since been considered his own. Quince was turning the Rafter T horse loose and examining the saddle he had bought. In the barn Webb paused, face dark in thought. "Quince, you were helpin' us the night

Clabe Donovan was broken out of jail. You saw him after Uncle Joe brought him down."

Quince nodded.

Webb said, "Would you say there was room for any doubt that it was Clabe Donovan we buried?"

Quince's eyes narrowed. "What're you gettin' at, Webb?"

Webb told him the whole story. Quince listened unbelievingly. "Webb, it can't be. And yet . . ." He was silent a moment, calling up old memories. "You know, his face *was* shot away. All we really had to go by was the size of him, and that black Mexican hat. And Uncle Joe swore it was him."

Webb said, "It was dark in that street. There was plenty of excitement. As for the hat, maybe one of the others picked it up in the jail. *Quién sabe?*"

"If Clabe Donovan had lived, why would he have stayed out of sight all these years? It wasn't his nature."

"Maybe he saw a chance to fade away, to get himself a fresh start."

"Then how come he would turn up now, outlawed again?"

"Could be he couldn't make it straight."

Quince Pyburn paced back and forth on the dirt floor of the barn, scowling in disbelief.

Webb said, "I don't want to believe it either, Quince. But we can't ignore what's happened. There's got to be an explanation."

"If we didn't kill Clabe Donovan, then who's that buried out yonder?"

Webb shrugged. "One of Clabe's *compadres*. Maybe even his brother Morg. They always looked a lot alike."

Quince dropped his thin frame upon a bale of hay. For a while he sat nervously flexing his hands, his face twisted. "If it *is* Clabe—and mind you, I'm not sayin' it is him come back to life—there's a bunch of us around here got to start watchin' our step. There's a bunch of us he swore he'd kill."

"Includin' you, Quince. And *me!*"

*   *   *

Most of the buildings on the street had low wooden porches, but between them there was only the dirt. Webb walked in the edge of the street itself, preferring that to stepping on and off the porches.

His living quarters—what there was of them—were in the long, narrow rock jail building beside the courthouse. He walked through the office into the small room where he kept his cot. He gathered up a change of clothes and walked out again. The doors of his two cells were swung open, the way he had left them. The only prisoner he had had was one *vaquero* arrested for fighting, and Webb had turned him loose before starting out toward the Box L.

He angled across the street to the barber shop, pausing in front of its peppermint-striped sign to glance at the Dry Fork Cafe. He didn't see Ellie Donovan. It was just as well, he thought.

What he had to tell her was going to floor her, he knew. He would put it off awhile. Maybe later he would know what to say.

"Got some hot water, Syl?" he asked the barber. "I sure do need a bath."

The barber nodded. "Got a kettle on the stove in the back."

Webb enjoyed a long, leisurely soak in the shop's cast-iron tub. The warm water seemed to draw out some of the fatigue that weighted his shoulders. Finished, he put on clean clothes, transferring his badge to a clean shirt. He walked out front again and dropped into the barber chair. Without having to ask, the barber began whipping up a lather and applying it to Webb's face. Syl was bald, or almost so. It seemed to Webb that most of the barbers he had known didn't have much hair, and he idly wondered why.

Webb could tell that curiosity was burning a hole in the barber. Webb waited until Syl was through using the razor, then gave him a brief account of the chase and gunfight. He left out any reference to Clabe Donovan. There had to be some kind of explanation, he was sure. No use getting people stirred up.

Changing the subject, Webb asked, "Syl, have you seen anything of my kid brother?"

Syl was slow in answering. "Yes, I seen Sandy."

Webb didn't like the tone of the reply. "He been into somethin' again?"

The barber shrugged. "Just a little scrap last night. Young rooster like that, he plays rougher than us older folks."

Finished, Webb paid Syl and rolled up his dirty clothes. "Syl, what did Sandy do this time?"

"Nothin' too bad, really. It's apt to cost a little, though. Him and that Augie Brock kid he's always runnin' around with, they had a scrap with a couple of gamblers over at the Longhorn Bar last night. There was some furniture and windowglass broke. And I think maybe a gambler's head."

Webb groaned. There was always a gambler or two over at the Longhorn, and most of them needed their heads broken. But it wasn't Sandy's place to do it, he thought with irritation.

The sun was getting low. Webb glanced again at the cafe, then carried the bundle of clothes across the railroad tracks to an adobe house where the widow Sanchez had a misspelled sign posted: CLOTHS WASHING. The old woman made a fair living washing for some of the town's unattached Anglo men. That done, Webb walked back down the street to the Longhorn Bar. It was an adobe building about twenty feet wide and some forty feet long. Lanterns, not lighted yet, hung on either side of the door and one more out at the edge of the porch roof's overhang. Webb noted that one of the front window glasses was missing.

A Mexican swamper pushed the swinging door open and swept dirt out into the street. He held the door for Webb and dropped his head slightly in deference. Inside, Webb paused to look around. The twelve-foot mahogany bar stood to the front, parallel to the left-hand wall. A big mirror with ornate wooden frame hung behind it. The bar and mirror had an expensive appearance out of place with the plastered adobe walls and the hard-packed dirt floor. The story was that Jake Scully had won them from another saloonkeeper in San Antonio in an all-night poker game.

Behind his bar, Scully polished glasses on his white towel

apron and frowned at Webb. "You hear what that brother of yours done in here last night?"

Cautiously Webb said, "I heard there was some kind of ruckus."

"Ruckus? More like a gangfight between a bunch of Irish railroaders. Them two boys, Sandy and Augie Brock, they came in here nosin' around. I could tell right off that they was trouble lookin' for a good place to happen. Things was kind of slow, and a couple of gamblers was sittin' back there havin' a quiet little game between theirselves. The boys, they asked to get in, and the gamblers said, 'Sure enough.' After a while Sandy jumped up and accused a gambler of pullin' a card out of his sleeve. It was hell amongst the yearlin's there for a little bit."

"Who won?"

"Them boys, I reckon you'd say. They was younger and a mite the liveliest. I finally had to cool that Brock button with a bung-starter. This mornin' both gamblers left town." Jake frowned deeply. "I sure did hate to see them go. They was payin' me a right nice percentage for the use of the place."

Webb pulled out his wallet. "How much you figure the damage comes to, Jake?"

Jake looked hungrily at Webb's money. "Well, they busted up a table, but I can fix that. It's been busted before. No charge. Then there's three chairs, gone beyond recall. Two dollars apiece—they wasn't plumb new. Boys, they busted four bottles of good whisky back there behind the bar, throwin' chairs. Two dollars apiece for them—all I'll ask is wholesale. Then there's this here mirror. They busted a corner out of it, and it'll never be as pretty as it was. I expect twenty dollars would be fair for the mirror. And, oh yes, the front window."

"I reckon they tossed a chair through that?"

"No, they threw out one of them gamblers, right through the glass." Jake frowned. "He never did come back in. Come to think of it, he owed me for a couple of drinks. But I reckon it ain't fair to charge you for that."

Webb shook his head. "No, I don't guess it is." He counted

on his fingers. "Jake, I'll take you at your word on this, all
except about that mirror. I happen to remember that corner
bein' busted out before. I'll give you twenty-five dollars.
That ought to cover it."

Jake Scully grimaced. "Now, Webb, I was kind of figurin'
it would run more than that."

"I oughtn't to pay you anything, you tryin' to get by me
with that mirror. But I'll give you twenty-five dollars if
you'll call it square."

Scully took the money, grunting as he counted it. "Don't
hold it agin me, Webb, me tryin' to get you to pay for that
mirror. It was broke by a couple of drunks in here a while
back. It was really your fault in a way. You're supposed to
keep the peace."

Webb said, "When they get to drinkin' that stuff you sell,
they're bound to bust somethin'."

Webb started toward the door. Jake Scully said, "Sheriff,
mind if I give you a little advice?"

"Shoot."

Scully fingered the money. "That boy has come of age,
Webb. It's time he found out a man's got to pay for his own
breakage. You keep on payin' him out of scrapes, he'll keep
causin' you trouble."

Webb said, "I'll take care of Sandy."

Dusk was settling over Dry Fork, bringing a fresh and pleasant coolness. As Webb left the saloon, the Mexican swamper
was lighting the lanterns to have them aglow before darkness
came. Jake Scully wouldn't want thirsty riders to pass by
and miss seeing his place.

From down the street Webb heard someone start picking
out a Mexican melody on a guitar, and he heard a thin voice
begin to lift with it. He stopped in front of the cafe and
glanced through the window to see if Ellie Donovan had any
customers. She didn't.

He stepped inside. "Hello, Ellie."

She turned, her face lighting as she saw him. She was a
woman of thirty, or perhaps a little less. Like Webb, she had

seen much of trouble, and it had left its stamp in her face, its mark in her eyes. She had been beaten and crushed but had risen again to stand upon her own feet with a stoic dignity. To Webb, she was still one of the prettiest women he had ever seen.

Ellie moved out from behind the counter. She gripped Webb's arms and tiptoed to kiss him. He started to put his arms around her but caught himself. Ellie was instantly aware that he was troubled.

"What is it, Webb?" She peered intently into his face. He avoided looking into her eyes. She said, "I saw you bring in a saddled horse." It was meant as a question.

"We had to kill a man," he replied.

She nodded soberly, looking away a moment. "No wonder you've got trouble riding on your shoulders. Sit down, Webb. I'll bring you some coffee. Want me to pour something extra into it?"

He shook his head and sat at a table. Ellie set down a steaming cup of black coffee. She moved around to stand beside him, her hand on his shoulder. "Been a long time since you've had to do that, Webb. I know you wouldn't have done it if it could have been avoided at all. You shouldn't let it get you down."

He glanced up at her a moment and was grateful for the gentle understanding in her eyes. Yet, there was a lot she didn't know about this, not yet. There was so much more he had to tell her. How could he say it?

Not long ago Webb had asked Ellie to marry him, and she had said yes. He was in the process of buying a house from a merchant who had sold out his business here and was moving to San Antonio.

Now . . .

Webb's mind drifted far back into memory. He had come to this part of the country when he was only about fifteen, hunting a ranch job. His father, a sheriff farther east, had been killed while trying to make an arrest. Webb had figured his mother would have a hard enough time trying to earn a living for herself and his five-year-old brother Sandy. He had gotten the ranch job, and he had sent most of the money home. Life had seemed terribly hard to him in those days.

He remembered the first time he had met Clabe Donovan.
Clabe was a couple of years older than Webb. He still had
both parents, but he had run off and left them. Now he was
hanging around with a wild bunch along the river. He always
seemed to have plenty of money without showing much sign
of having to work for it. Webb had liked Clabe in those days,
and he had been sorely tempted to follow Clabe's example.
Ranch work was long and hard and didn't pay much for a
kid.

It had even reached the point that Webb was supposed to
meet Clabe one night and ride off with the bunch on some
mysterious expedition. Webb hadn't known then just what
the plan was, but he had known it was something lawless.
Webb's father and mother had taught him a strong sense of
values, had pounded into him their solid belief that it was
no disgrace to be poor if one was honest and of good conscience. Webb had ridden to the rendezvous point with those
voices of old ringing in his ears. And when Clabe had come,
Webb had pulled back into the shadows and hidden from
him.

Days later, Webb heard of a bank robbery 70 miles away,
a robbery in which a bank teller and an outlaw were killed.
The outlaw had been a kid holding the robbers' horses.

That, Webb had realized, would have been his job if he
had gone.

When Webb was about twenty, his mother died. It became
Webb's duty to take his little brother under his wing. Because Webb had been a level-headed youth and a crack shot,
the sheriff had offered him a job as deputy. Lawing paid
better than cowboying. With a brother to care for, Webb had
accepted. He had worn a badge ever since. He had tried to
take good care of Sandy and teach him the lessons his mother
would have taught if she had lived.

As for Clabe Donovan, he had slipped irretrievably beyond
the pale. He had become an expert border jumper, keeping
himself out of the hands of the law on both sides of the river.
Most of his depredations were on the Texas side, where he
could go back across to sanctuary. True, there was law in

Mexico, too, but it was a big and wild country across there. Its law-enforcement agencies were not so well developed, not well equipped, nor did they have much incentive to go against Clabe. After all, Clabe caused little trouble on their side, and he *did* bring back considerable amounts of money which he spread around with complete abandon. Easy come, easy go. And money was not easy to come by in Mexico.

Like Webb Matlock, Clabe Donovan had had a younger brother. While Webb had been trying to teach Sandy to ride a straight road, Clabe had taught Morg Donovan the twisted ways of a crooked trail. It had not been hard to do, for by natural bent Morg took to the lawless ways like a duck to water.

The brothers' daring had brought them a grudging respect, if not a liking, among many of the border settlers—those the Donovans had not yet bothered.

It had been significant to Webb that the people who spoke with sympathy of the Donovans had never been their victims. And those who did feel some admiration for them usually changed readily enough when they had seen the outlaws in a new light—say, over the muzzle of a gun. That took the romance out of it.

Once Clabe and Morg had dropped out of sight for more than a year. Rumor had it that they had been cut down while trying to steal golden ornaments from a cathedral far down in Mexico. But it turned out later they had simply gone west under assumed names. Clabe had taken a notion he wanted a simpler life. He had found Ellie and married her, the girl having no idea what he had been. Before long, the old restlessness came over him again. One night he and Morg had spurred home on sweat-lathered horses, anxiously watching their backtrail. They had drageed the dismayed Ellie Donovan with them back to this part of the country.

Sickening of a hideout life across the river, her dreams and illusions shattered, she had ridden away one night while the Donovans were gone. She had wound up in Dry Fork. Here she had found hostility from some but sympathy from many more. Among the sympathetic was Webb Matlock.

Webb had fallen in love with Ellie a long time ago. Lately,

with Clabe Donovan thought dead and that nightmare gradually receding into the past, Ellie had begun to return Webb's
love.

Now . . .

"Ellie," Webb said regretfully, "I got somethin' to tell you.
It may not be true . . . I can't believe it is. But *if* it is, I want
you to hear it first from me, not from the gossip of the street."

He told her what had happened. As she listened, Ellie's
face drained of color. Both hands went up over her eyes.
When finally she brought the hands down, Webb could see
that her eyes brimmed with tears.

"Clabe, alive?" Her voice quavered. "How, Webb? How?"

He shook his head. "Like I told you, Ellie, it may not be
true. For my sake—and for yours—I hope it's not."

She lowered her chin. A tear ran slowly down her check.
"But if it is, I'm still married to him."

"You could get a divorce, Ellie. There's not a court in the
country wouldn't give it to you and say you deserved it."

She clasped her hands together. "When I married him, I
made a promise—for better or for worse."

"He broke all the promises he ever made to you."

"I made my promise to God, not to Clabe Donovan."
Pushing to her feet, she took a handkerchief from a pocket
in her apron. She turned her back to Webb, but he could see
her shoulders tremble. She touched the handkerchief to her
eyes. Webb put his hand on her shoulders and turned her
around, pulling her to him so that her bowed head touched
his chest.

"Ellie . . ."

She pulled away. "Webb, this changes a lot of things."

"What do you mean?"

"Until we know for sure, we can't see each other the way
we've been doing. Our marriage is off, Webb. It *has* to be.
And you'd better not visit me at home anymore. It wouldn't
be proper."

Regretfully he said, "All right, Ellie."

She sat down at one of the tables, her body stiff from
shock, the handkerchief gripped so tightly that her right hand
was almost white.

"Pull down the shades for me, Webb. I don't feel like serving anybody else tonight."

He pulled down the shades and paused a moment at the door, looking back at her with his heart aching. She dropped her head into her arms and began to cry.

"Good night, Ellie," he said.

She couldn't answer and didn't try. He pulled the door shut and walked down the street, his shoulders slumped.

In his office Webb lighted a lamp, rolled up the top of his desk and sat down. From his shirtpocket he took the worn letter he had found on the dead boy. He smoothed it out and laboriously copied onto a fresh envelope the smudged return address. It was in such poor condition that he had to work it out letter by letter:

On a sheet of white paper he began to write:

Dear Mrs. Brill:

It becomes my most painful duty to write and inform you of the death of your son James. He was working on the Box L Ranch when a horse fell on him. He lived only long enough to ask us to write and tell you he loved you. Your son had not been here long, but he was well liked. He was a hard worker.

Webb took out a few bills he had found in the boy's pocket and placed them with the money Quince had given him for the saddle and gun. It was not very much, he thought. Remembering his own mother and her constant need, he opened his own wallet and removed most of the money he had left in it. He placed these bills with the others.

Your son had some wages due him, and his employer asked me to forward them to you. Also, we took the liberty of selling his saddle. The proceeds are enclosed herewith. My deepest sympathies to you in this time of bereavement.

Your most sympathetic servant,
Webb Matlock, sheriff.

Webb had started to write the words "and gun" after "saddle" but caught himself. He folded the letter with the money inside it, stuck it into the envelope and sealed the flap. He put a stamp on it so it would be ready to mail as soon as he got over to the postoffice.

He blew out the lamp and sat awhile in the darkness, thinking about Clabe Donovan, wondering why a boy like this James Brill would have gotten himself tied up with a wild bunch, why he had to die just when his life should have been beginning to reach its fulfillment. Webb knew the answer, for he had heard the same wild call himself once. It was the call to which Clabe Donovan had responded years ago, a call to which he had hopelessly abandoned himself.

Once over the edge that way, it was hard ever to come back. A majority of them never wanted to.

Brooding to himself, Webb didn't hear the girl come silently into his office. She spoke, and he jerked himself aright. "Birdie! You gave me a jolt."

Birdie Hanks, just turned seventeen, apologized. "I didn't mean to scare you, Webb. I just wondered if you've seen Sandy."

He shook his head. "Not since I left here day before yesterday."

She said worriedly, "He hasn't been around. I wondered if I'd done or said something to make him mad."

Another time, Webb would have smiled. He liked this slender, guileless girl with her honey-colored hair done in braids, the bloom of womanhood just beginning to touch her. An older woman would not have asked so directly. She would have taken ten minutes in working around the question, asking it but at the same time not asking.

"He's at an ornery age, Birdie," Webb said. "He's just commenced to feel his manhood, and he's not right sure what to do about it. He doesn't know what he wants to make of himself, whichaway to jump. Most boys go through it, and they come out all right. Don't you worry."

"I heard about that fight he got into last night. It caused a real commotion over at my house. Dad says Sandy's too wild for me, wants me to stop seeing him."

Webb frowned, placing his fingertips together. Sandy *was* getting a reputation. Webb didn't know what to do about it. Talking didn't seem to help much anymore. He figured the boy would just have to thrash it out for himself—with a little helpful push here and there.

"Birdie, Sandy has had to grow up without the guidance that most boys get. I've had to try to be both daddy and mother to him, and I really wasn't either one. Some of the lessons, I've pounded into him. Some of them, though, I never have been able to make him take. Maybe someday a woman can teach him the rest. You might be that woman."

Birdie sat sideways in a cane-bottomed chair, one arm over the back of it, her chin resting on the arm. Wistfully she said, "I'd like to be."

He rolled a cigarette and licked the edge of the paper to make it stick. "I hope you will. You're a good girl, Birdie. I like you."

"I like you, too, Webb. I wish Sandy could be more like you."

Webb felt a glow of pride in the compliment. "He'll be all right, Birdie. We've just got to have patience."

She nodded and stood up. As she started toward the door, Webb said, "Glad you came by. I'll tell Sandy you were here."

She shook her head. "Don't. I don't want to give him that satisfaction."

It was warm in his office. With so much on his mind, Webb knew it would be futile to try to go to bed and sleep. He pulled a chair out onto the little wooden porch and leaned back in the darkness to feel the south breeze that had cooled with the night and to listen to the lulling night sounds of the town. It was a quiet town, a low murmur of talk coming from one of the bars. From another came the plaintive picking of a Mexican guitar. Somewhere a baby cried, and a cow bawled for a calf.

At length Webb heard footsteps. He could recognize

Sandy by his way of walking as the young man approached the front of the jail. Sandy didn't see Webb until the sheriff spoke.

"Hello, Sandy."

Sandy jerked in surprise and stopped to stare. "That you, Webb?"

"It's me. Got back this afternoon."

"Heard you did. Heard you got one of them." Webb felt a hint of resentment in his brother's voice.

"He was a kid, Sandy, no older than you are. Even a little younger, I'd say."

"I wanted to go. I tried to get you to take me." The resentment was bold and open now.

"I told you *no*. That's all there was to it. Just be glad you weren't there." A testiness crept into Webb's tone. Seemed almost any discussion he had with Sandy anymore worked into an argument.

Sandy demanded, "Why? Tell me why you won't let me go with you. Tell me why you won't deputize me when you've got somethin' like that."

Tiredly Webb said, "Sandy, I've told you before. You know, so why keep on askin'?"

He stared at his brother. He couldn't make him out in the night, but he could let his imagination fill in what he couldn't see. Sandy was almost as tall as Webb but lighter in weight. He had the quick, easy movement of the very young, an erect stance and walk that bespoke a fierce pride. He had a self-assurance that with a little coaxing could almost become arrogance. He was quick to laugh, quick to flare into anger. As a boy he had sometimes said things in the heat of argument that he later regretted. But rather than apologize or take them back, he would fight to uphold them. Even now, he probably had more fist fights than anybody in Dry Fork.

Up to now this quick temper had made it hard for him to hold a steady ranch job. Sooner or later he would swell up and come to blows with one of the other hands and either quit or be sent back to town. Most of the time he did "day work," temporary jobs at roundup time or on short cattle drives. A good hand with horses, he picked up some money breaking and training broncs.

Sandy stubbornly pressed the issue. "All right, Webb, tell me again how come you don't want me along as a deputy?"

Pushing back a grating impatience, Webb said, "In the first place, you're my own brother. I couldn't hire you steady because people would say I was usin' my office to put my family on the county payroll."

"All right, so you can't hire me steady. But you could occasionally swear me in when you need extra help, like the other day. I could at least be gettin' the experience."

"Experience for what? What could it lead to? I don't know a single job where posse experience would be worth two cents Mexican money to you."

"I want to be a lawman, Webb."

Webb let his leaned-back chair tip forward, the front legs thumping solidly on the porch. "Boy, we've been through that before. It's foolishness. A lawman's life is no damned good. I'd sooner see you out with a wagon, gatherin' up cow bones."

"*You* haven't done so bad at it. You haven't been killed yet."

Webb started to say *I'm still young*, but he didn't feel that it was exactly true. Young in years, perhaps, but not in experience. And tonight he felt old. He said, "It killed our father, Sandy. It's a dirty business sometimes, a dirty, bloody business. Like yesterday, us havin' to shoot that kid. I got enough on my conscience already. Do you think I want to see you have to go carryin' things like that around? Stick to your cowboying."

Sandy said, "I'm gettin' too old for you to keep on tellin' me what to do."

"You're not near as old as you think you are."

"I'm already older than you were when they first pinned a deputy badge on you."

Webb felt a compulsion to say, *Then for God's sake act like it!* But he held it down. "Sandy," he said evenly, "some people just take a lot longer to grow up than others do. You haven't got there yet."

Times he wondered if Sandy ever would.

Sandy argued, "I can take care of myself—always did. You just try me one time, that's all I ask. Just one time. I heard who-all was on that posse from the Box L. Men like Uncle Joe Vickers, so old and stiff he can't hardly get on a horse anymore. And Ollie Reed. If there's anyone who's got less business on a posse than Ollie Reed, I'd hate to see him. I sure couldn't be any worse than some of that bunch."

Impatience needling him, Webb responded, "They're all grown men, and they've got grown men's judgment. Their bodies may move slow, but their minds are quick enough. They won't pull some sudden fool stunt and get themselves or somebody else killed."

Sandy began to bristle. "And you think I would?"

"I think you might. The way you act around here, I'd be afraid to trust you."

Sandy's fists clenched. Webb knew that if it had been anyone besides himself, Sandy would have been ready to fight. They'd had plenty of arguments, but they had never fought each other.

Sandy said, "I'm no baby, and one of these days I'll prove it to you." He strode past Webb and went into the office. He lighted a lamp, the yellow glow spilling out the open door onto the porch. In a couple of minutes he was back with a roll of blankets under one arm, his war-bag of clothes and belongings in the other.

Webb demanded, "Where you goin'?"

Sandy glared at him. "I got a job breakin' some colts. I had figured on goin' out in the mornin'. Now I think I'll just ride on out tonight."

"Don't act like a six-year-old kid who's had his cookies taken away from him! There's no sense startin' out in the dark."

"Then maybe I'll sleep in Quince's wagonyard. I sure don't aim to stay here."

"Cool off, Sandy. Show some sense."

"*You* show some." Sandy stepped off the porch and stomped down the street, quickly passing beyond the weak glow of the lamp. Webb stood up and watched him go, wanting to call him back and try to reason with him. But what was the use? He couldn't reason with Sandy much anymore. The boy had a head as hard as that of a freighter's mule.

They had argued like this before, and other times Sandy had left in anger. He always came back.

But what if one day he left and didn't come back?

3

SOMETIME THAT NIGHT OLLIE REED GOT TO DRINKING AND unhinged his tongue. By morning the story about Clabe Donovan was all over town. A dozen people came into Webb's office while he was trying to finish some paperwork. For each of them he had to tell all over again what he knew, what he believed and didn't believe.

"I'm not satisfied yet that it is Clabe," he said. "Don't stand to reason that a man would come back after all these years when everybody thought he was dead. But then, Clabe never was a reasonable sort of a man."

The interruption Webb really hated to see coming was Judge Upshaw. The judge was a pompous, middle-aged man who in this hot weather was wearing a black vest with a golden watch chain hanging across his ample belly. He stopped in the door and looked down his nose at Webb.

"What's this foolishness going around town about Clabe Donovan?" he demanded.

Coolly Webb said, "I don't know what you've heard."

"You know. And I think you ought to arrest any man who gets drunk and goes around telling tales like that to scare people. There isn't a word of truth in it!" He paused, eyebrows lifting hopefully. "Is there?"

With forced patience Webb told him what he had told all the others.

"Preposterous!" the judge snorted. "Preposterous!" but doubt seemed to crowd into his eyes. "What if it *were* true, though? Think of all the people Clabe Donovan threatened. He even threatened *me!*"

Webb nodded. "That's right, judge. He sure did. You said some mighty hard things about him when you sentenced him to hang. And he said some hard things back at you."

The judge had only been in the county a couple of years when Clabe had been tried. At that time he and Webb still got along fairly well. But they had drawn apart since. Upshaw had tried to use his office to do some personal land grabbing. Webb had stopped him by throwing his hired toughs in jail or by escorting them to the county line. Webb had no use for the man now. But the judge had gotten himself re-elected. He still had that much political power, although he hadn't been able to beat Webb with one of his own hand-picked candidates for sheriff.

It was a stand-off, the way it looked now.

Upshaw said sharply, "Matlock, it's your job to find out if Clabe Donovan *is* alive. If he is, it's up to you to bring him in. And I hope you bring him dead!"

By the time Webb got started for the Rafter T ranch, much of the morning was gone. At the livery barn he slipped a rope halter on the bay horse the young outlaw had been riding. He headed south, leading the horse in a steady trot.

The summer sun bore down with uncompromising hostility. Not even a cotton-puff cloud was in sight to promise a moment's shade and relief. But Webb Matlock had been born to this kind of country, raised in it so that he hardly knew any other kind of country existed. He was aware of the heat, but he took it in stride and did not waste time or emotion cursing it. He soon started to sweat, and now and then a breeze came searching across the rolling prairie to make the wet shirt feel cool against his skin.

For such little favors he was grateful, but his mind was on things more important than the heat.

The rolling prairie broke off into rough, rocky hills, criss-crossed by draws and rough headers. Some of these draws were wide and covered by knee-high grass. The grass was

brown now from summer heat, but it had made good growth
earlier, and though brown it had considerable strength. Fall
rains, if they came, would put green back into the grass in
time to rebuild its value for winter grazing before frost came.
This thick grass would lie there all winter, cured and strong,
like hay on the ground.

Good country for a horse outfit. Or cattle. Webb had a few
cattle of his own grazing on free range north of town. He
wished he had some land like this, bought and paid for. This
was Bronc Tomlin's country, paid in cash. Nobody ever
knew where Tomlin got the money. When he had come here
fifteen years ago he hadn't seemed the kind to have earned
so much honestly. But he had it, and nobody thought it ju-
dicious to ask questions. His money spent as good as anyone
else's, when he spent any. Most of the time Bronc Tomlin
stayed home and minded his business.

Webb came upon a small band of mares with colts, and a
stallion moved forward to look him over. Webb made a
healthy circle, for sometimes these old studs could be mean.
When the stallion came close, Webb took off his hat and
waved it, hollering. The animal moved away, and Webb
breathed easier. The stud and all the mares, he had noted, bore
the Rafter T brand, same as this bay the young outlaw had ridden.

When he came in sight of the ranch headquarters, Webb
stopped. He stepped to the ground and stretched a moment,
for he had been in the saddle a long time. He reached into
his saddlebags and brought out a couple of cans. One was a
flat tin of sardines, the other a can of tomatoes. He opened
them with a heavy blade of his pocketknife and squatted in
the grass to eat. He would like to have had bread and coffee,
but they weren't practical to carry on a ride like this. He
could do without. A man could make out on sardines and
tomatoes now and again. It was well past noon. Even if it
hadn't been, Webb didn't want to ask or accept any favors
from Bronc Tomlin.

Sitting there, he studied the ranch layout. There weren't
any womenfolks on the Rafter T, at least not on a steady
basis. Once in a while old Bronc found himself a saloon girl

who thought she wanted some fresh air, and he would take her out there a little while. Most of them didn't stay long. Tomlin's ranchhouse was built of rock, solid but not designed for looks. As far as Webb could remember, none of the windows had ever seen a curtain. He couldn't make it out from here, but Webb could remember the junk pile of rusted tin cans and whisky bottles just back of the house. Bronc Tomlin had strung wire around it to keep his horses from straying in and cutting their feet. That made it no less of an eyesore. Bronc had an eye for beauty in horses, but he wasn't particular about the place he lived in. Anything with a roof over it suited him. Like many another old open-range man who had spent years sleeping out under the stars, Bronc Tomlin was easily satisfied in that respect.

Riding in, Webb had to get down and open a wire gate leading into a small horse pasture where Tomlin could keep several horses within easy reach. Most of his horses ran on the unfenced range. The bay Webb was leading nickered at some young horses nearby, and the horses came up in friendly curiosity.

Webb could see activity in a circular corral, where dust stirred restlessly. He could see the outline of a man bobbing up and down, riding a pitching bronc. Webb could hear shouts of encouragement and knew other men were in the corral afoot. He started to ride that way, then reined around. He spotted Bronc Tomlin standing on the front porch of the rock house. Webb touched spurs to his own horse and rode over to Tomlin.

Tomlin leaned lazily against a porch post, rolling a cigarette. He nodded at Webb but devoted most of his attention to a horseman's appraisal of the sheriff's mount. Then his gaze drifted back to the bay Webb was leading.

"By George," he exclaimed, "that there's one of my horses."

Dryly Webb said, "It sure is."

The rancher pushed himself away from the post and stepped down to look the horse over. Tomlin was well into his fifties, a freckle-faced, heavy-moving man with a soft belly sagging over his belt. His clothes were dirty. His graying hair bushed out from beneath a greasy old hat. He hadn't had a haircut in months, nor had he shaved lately. No woman out here right now, Webb would bet.

Tomlin walked around the bay, patting the animal, lifting up one forefoot and looking at it. "Has a tendency to lame easy, this one does. Been limpin' any?"

"Not that I could see," Webb replied, waiting to hear what kind of explanation Tomlin would have. He figured the man was stalling for time, thinking up a good story.

"Been missin' this horse for three or four weeks now. Him and six others, they just disappeared. I ran onto a cowboy who'd seen them—said he'd accidently ridden onto some tough-lookin' hombres camped down on the river with my horses. I decided I didn't really need them very much. Man can't figure on keepin' them all."

Webb studied the man's face. "They stole those horses, did they?"

"I sure didn't give 'em away!"

"How come you didn't report it to me?"

Tomlin shrugged. "Look, sheriff, I'm off down here to-ward the river, a long ways from town. Any of them border outlaws really wanted to, they could wipe me off the map in one good sweep. I ain't a-lookin' for no trouble with them. If the worst they do is pick up a horse now and again, I don't figure I'm bad off. I'll just look on that kind of like a tax and leave things be."

Webb eyed him narrowly. "You don't appear to me to be afraid of an occasional outlaw, Bronc."

"I ain't afraid, exactly. But what's the sense in a man goin' out in the dark with his lamp lit, huntin' trouble? I go my own way, mind my own business and don't cause nobody any worry."

Webb said dryly, "You cause some worry, all right." He didn't believe Bronc, but what could he prove? "Sometimes a man who stands by and does nothing can be as much help to an outlaw like Clabe Donovan as somebody who really pitches in with him."

Tomlin looked up sharply. "What do you mean, Clabe Donovan? He's been dead a long time."

Webb watched the man closely for any betrayal, any loss of composure. "Has he, Bronc?"

Suddenly ill at ease, Tomlin said, "Sheriff, I got no idea what you're hintin' at."

"I think you do, Bronc."

Tomlin said, "I ain't done nothin' illegal, sheriff. And if I had, you couldn't prove it on me."

"I'm not accusin' you of anything, Bronc. I just came to bring you your horse." *And*, he thought, *to look around a little*.

Bronc Tomlin usually kept from six to ten hands around. Webb could see sign of only three right now, the three in the corral where the broncs were being worked.

He stepped down from the saddle and handed the halter rein to Tomlin. "Halter belongs to Quince. I better take it back."

Tomlin nodded, pushing aside any resentment he might have felt. "We'll go turn him into a corral." They walked side by side. Tomlin said, "Sure do thank you, sheriff, for bringin' me my horse. Maybe some of the others will turn up eventually."

Webb didn't pay much attention because he was sure Tomlin was lying anyway. He listened to a murmur of talk out in the circular corral and a pounding of hoofs as a bronc broke into pitching. Webb decided to see what Tomlin's helpers looked like. He thought he could still recognize a couple or three of the old Donovan bunch on sight.

A man never knew until he tried.

Several young broncs were haltered and tied along the fence outside the circular corral. Inside, a brown horse pitched with a saddle. The men were letting him work himself down before they mounted him. Webb could make out two men in the center of the pen, their backs to him. A third leaned against a fence so that Webb could see nothing of him but the color of his clothes between the planks.

One of the cowboys half turned and said over his shoulder, "All right, Sandy, let's see you top him."

Webb stopped in midstride. Sandy?

He climbed up on the fence for a look. He saw Sandy's

friend, young Augie Brock, working up the taut rope and grabbing the bronc by the ears. In panic the bronc tried to paw him, but Augie held himself close to the horse's body and swung with agility. "Come on, Sandy," he said, "hurry it up."

Sandy Matlock strode confidently out into the stirring dust. The bronc tried to kick him, but Sandy stepped quickly aside. He stuck his left foot into the stirrup, gripped the reins up short and swung aboard. "Let 'er rip!"

Augie Brock turned loose and jumped back out of the way. The bronc humped its back and lunged forward. Leather popped as the brown jumped and twisted. The hoofs raised clouds of dust. Sandy Matlock sat in full control, swaying with the violent motion, keeping the hackamore rein loose, and giving the bronc all the freedom it wanted. He wasn't spurring, for it would only make the horse pitch harder. That might have been good for a show, but it wasn't worth much in training a horse for useful purpose.

Webb watched with pride, for he knew Sandy was one of the best bronc riders in this part of the country, a better one than Webb had ever been. Each man to his own talents.

Sandy let the bronc pitch until it began to tire. Then he started drawing up the hackamore rein, firmly pulling the pony's head higher. With its head up, a horse cannot do a good job of pitching. Once the brown had gotten its fill and found the rider unshaken, it began to run aimlessly around and around the corral. Sandy let it run awhile, then began pulling the rein first one way, then the other. The horse did not respond well to the rein, but that would come. It was part of the training.

Finally Sandy stepped down and walked away laughing, his legs wobbly from fatigue. It was hard work handling one of these broncs.

"I'm goin' to need me some coffee before I climb on the next one," he said to Augie Brock.

Webb and Tomlin had watched without saying anything to one another. Sandy had had his hands too full to notice Webb. Now, walking toward the gate, he saw him. He stopped, his grin turning quickly into a frown.

"What're you doin' here, Webb?"

Webb said, "I was fixin' to ask you the same thing."

"I told you I had me a job breakin' some broncs."

"You didn't tell me it was here."

"No reason I ought to've."

Bronc Tomlin said, "This boy in some kind of trouble, sheriff? I sure don't want no trouble out here."

Webb shook his head. "He's not in trouble. And he's not goin' to stay here and get in any."

Belligerently Sandy said to Webb, "I don't know as you've got any say about it."

Tomlin squinted at Sandy Matlock, "You know, boy, I don't believe Augie ever told me your name. Who are you?"

Webb answered the question. "His name is Sandy Matlock. He's my brother."

Tomlin's eyes widened for a second. "Your brother?" He peered intently at Sandy. "I ought to've known it, but its been so long since I saw the button, and he's growed a right smart." Tomlin glanced at Augie Brock. "Why didn't you tell me this here boy was the sheriff's brother?"

Augie shrugged. He was a tall kid with a crooked-toothed grin and a heavy shock of reddish hair pushing out from under his hat. "Never thought about it. Didn't know it would make any difference."

Tomlin said, "It don't, to me. But seems like it does to the sheriff."

Webb nodded at Sandy. "Get your stuff together. You're goin' back with me."

Sandy flushed. "Not this time."

Webb stiffened. "Sandy . . ." The one word was enough, the firm way he said it.

Bronc Tomlin watched, a flicker of malice in his eyes. He asked Sandy, "How old are you, boy?"

Sandy replied, "Old enough!"

"Then stay if you want to. This ain't no sheriff matter, and Webb's got no more rights over you as a brother."

This, then, was a challenge from Tomlin, a challenge to be met only through Sandy. Webb knew he could not hesitate. He took Sandy's arm and pulled his brother forward. "Come on!"

Sandy hauled back. For a moment he glared at Webb, then Webb saw the intention flare in the young man's eyes. Sandy crouched, his fist suddenly coming up. Webb swung aside, taking the blow on his shoulder. Sandy was strong. Webb staggered back, thrown off balance.

Well, he thought, *it's been a long time working up to this. Now we'll get it over and done with.*

He didn't want to fight Sandy, but he knew he had to, now. He just wanted to get it finished the quickest way he could. He stepped in close and swung hard. His fist struck Sandy a glancing blow across the ribs, for Sandy had twisted away. Grunting, Sandy drove a hard right into Webb's chin. Pain hammered through Webb's brain. He staggered again.

Sandy was stouter than he had thought.

Sandy followed up with a vengeance, trying again to connect with Webb's chin. Webb warded off the blow with his left arm and put his whole weight into a hard right to Sandy's stomach. Sandy grunted as the breath went out of him. Webb struck him again, this time with the left.

They stood toe to toe and swapped blows, each man putting all he had in it. It was a cruel beating for both of them. They wore themselves down in a stubborn stand. Neither tried very hard to duck what the other had to give him. Each attempted only to hit harder than the other.

Sandy's youth had given him endurance, but Webb's weight gave the sheriff power. Even as he himself tired, Webb sensed that Sandy was wearing faster.

Webb tried to keep from hitting the kid in the face. He drove his fists into Sandy's body, swinging, punching, pushing, and punching again. Sandy was gasping, the breath almost gone from him. He swayed, he staggered, and at last he sank to his knees. He knelt there with his head down, struggling hard for breath.

Breathing hard, swaying too, Webb reached down for his brother's arm. "Come on, Sandy."

In a last rush of anger, Sandy pushed up off his knees and swung again at Webb. Webb stepped back. The blow missed him, and Sandy flopped belly down on the ground.

Webb knew it was over.

He stood a while, fighting to get his breath back. His shirt was torn half off, the sleeve hanging down from the elbow. He was soaked in sweat, and dust clung to him. The salty taste of dust and sweat and blood was on his lips.

When he was able, Webb stepped behind his brother and helped him to his feet. "We're goin', button. Make up your mind to that."

Tomlin watched, frowning but keeping hands off. "That boy come within an inch of whippin' you, Webb. He's grown but you won't admit it."

Webb wanted to tell him to mind his own business, but he had no breath yet to waste in talking.

Tomlin said, "Some day, Webb, you got to cut the cord."

Webb found Sandy's horse and saddled him. Silently Augie Brock brought out Sandy's blankets, still rolled up the way Sandy had carried them here. Webb tied them behind Sandy's saddle. He glanced at Augie. "How about you? You goin' in with us?"

Augie gave him a hard, challenging grin. "You're *his* brother, not mine."

Webb shrugged, seeing no point in arguing with him. He turned to Sandy. "Can you get up by yourself, or do you need help?"

Sandy glared, one eye beginning to darken. He put his foot in the stirrup and painfully pulled himself up without accepting assistance.

Tomlin stood with hands shoved deep into his pockets, his eyes unfriendly. "What's the matter with us out here, sheriff? We got smallpox or somethin'?"

Firmly Webb said, "You know what the matter is. I don't have to spell it out for you."

The dirty, bewhiskered old horseman stood and stared Webb in the eye. Finally he turned aside and spat a stream of tobacco juice. To Sandy he said, "Boy, any time you want to come back out here and work, you just do it."

Webb pulled away. Sandy followed along behind him.

For a long time they rode like that, Sandy trailing in a

surly mood. Finally Webb turned in the saddle and looked back at him. "What are you, an Indian, that you've got to ride single file?"

Sandy touched a spur to his horse and pulled up even with his brother. His jaw was swelling a little. It jutted in a smouldering anger. At length he demanded, "When you finally goin' to leave me alone? I was goin' to get good pay for ridin' them broncs."

"That's an outlaw bunch yonder, Sandy. You don't want to have nothin' to do with an outfit like that."

"I didn't see nothin' that looked shady to me."

"You would have if you'd stayed long enough, I expect. And you might've got yourself mixed up in it so you couldn't get out."

"I got two eyes of my own, and I got a brain, too. I can figure out what's best for me. I don't need your help."

"I wish I could believe that was so."

They rode in silence again, Sandy plainly doing some deep thinking. Finally he said, "I think you're all wet about that place. But if it *was* the truth, what did you leave Augie Brock out there for?"

Webb said grimly, "Augie's in just the kind of place where he belongs. If you haven't seen through him yet, I guess you never will."

4

ELLIE DONOVAN DAUBED AT THE REDDENING ABRASIONS on Webb's face, with a clean cloth wet with antiseptic. Webb flinched, breathing in a hissing sound between his teeth.

"At least you had the wounds cleaned," she said.

"We stopped at the creek and washed the dirt off."

"The creek?" Her voice was incredulous. "Probably let your horses drink out of it first, too. It'll be a wonder if you don't both get these place infected and die from it."

"We'll be all right."

Her scolding tone disappeared. Her voice became sympathetic. "It's a terrible thing, having to fight your own brother that way."

"I didn't want to, but I guess it's been a long time comin'. Now at least we got it over with."

She looked critically at a cut place. "Well, I hope he doesn't look any worse than you do. Where is Sandy, anyhow?"

"I don't rightly know. He cut away from me quick's we hit town."

"Why don't you hunt him and send him over here? I'll fix his face, too."

"He'll probably go to Birdie Hanks. She'll take care of

him. Anyway, he's not in bad shape. I avoided his face as much as I could."

Ellie went on quietly with the work, flinching each time Webb flinched, biting her lip when she caused him pain. Finally done, she leaned back and said, "I guess that will hold you. It's not the worst fight you were ever in, I suppose."

He said evenly, "It's the one I least wanted. But I couldn't let him stay out there, not in that outlaw bunch."

Ellie looked nervously at her hands, wanting to ask him a question but plainly dreading the answer he might give her. "Webb, did you . . . did you find out anything?"

He shook his head. "Not for sure. I fished for information, mentioned Clabe Donovan without any warning just to see if anything showed up in Bronc Tomlin's face. It surprised him, all right. But I couldn't tell if it was just that he hadn't thought about Clabe in a long time, or if he was surprised that I knew about Clabe bein' alive."

"Webb, are you sure he *is* alive? Are you sure we haven't all been jumping to some wrong conclusions?"

"I'm not sure of anything, Ellie. Nothin' at all." He took Ellie's hand. "Even if he *is* alive, you don't love him anymore. You couldn't."

Miserably Ellie said, "How can I answer you, Webb? I only know that when I left him I was still in love with him. I knew in my mind that I should hate him, but I couldn't. I left him because I couldn't stand the kind of life we were living, not because I didn't love him. Once I was away from him, I could tell that I was beginning to change. And after he was killed—or we *thought* he was killed—I finally had to close my mind to him, had to let him go. Now things are different again. Maybe I wouldn't love him anymore—probably wouldn't. But how can I know? Unless I really see him again, how can I ever know?"

Webb turned away, avoiding her eyes. Silent a while, he finally said, "I oughtn't to come here at all, Ellie. It'd be better for both of us if I didn't even see you till this thing was settled for once and for all. But I don't think I could get up the will power to stay away. I still want you as much as I ever did. Whatever happens won't change that."

* * *

He walked down to the doctor's house and knocked. Uncle Joe Vickers opened the door.

"Howdy, Uncle Joe. Came to see how Jess Leggett is gettin' along."

Joe Vickers answered loudly enough so he was sure the wounded rancher in the back room could hear. "The old reprobate's in better shape than he's got any right to be. The weller he gets, the meaner he is. If he was much meaner, he'd just bite himself and die. Come on in. Doctor's off on a call. Mexican woman sick the other side of town."

From the back room Webb could hear Jess Leggett call: "That you, Webb Matlock? You git yourself in here!"

Sitting up in his bed, the crusty old rancher scowled, "Where the hell you been?"

There hadn't been much today to smile about, but now Webb Matlock began to let himself go. "Your temperature must be all right, because your temper's back to normal. The better you feel, the harder you are for a man to get along with."

Jess Leggett said crisply, "I didn't ask you in here to insult me. I got men here who can do that better than you, and I'm payin' them." He nodded his chin toward Joe Vickers and the pleasant-faced young cowboy, Johnny Willet. "What happened to your face, Webb? You look like you came out second in a two-dog fight."

Webb shrugged it off. "I guess I did." He didn't tell Jess any more, and the old man seemed to sense that he wouldn't. The rancher asked, "What've you found out about them cow thieves?"

Webb told about his visit to the Bronc Tomlin place, but he left out his fight with Sandy.

Leggett demanded, "What about this foolishness bein' spread around town that Donovan's back in circulation? It's a lie, ain't it?"

Soberly Webb said, "I wish I could say for sure that it was. I'm not convinced yet that it's true. But it could be."

"Hogwash! I was there when they nailed the coffin shut."

"Could you see Clabe Donovan's face?"

Leggett frowned. "No, old Joe yonder did too good a job with his shotgun for that. But hell, everybody knew it was Clabe. There wasn't anybody had any doubt."

"Could be we were all wrong, Jess."

Gray-haired Joe Vickers straightened his bent shoulders. "I wasn't wrong, Webb. I swore it then and I'll swear it now: I shot Clabe Donovan!"

Webb shrugged. No use in a man arguing with somebody who was that sure about something, especially when Webb didn't want to believe it anyway. He changed the subject.

"That shoulder hurtin' you much, Jess?"

"A slug in the shoulder won't kill me. I fought in the Mexican War, and I've lived on the border the biggest part of my life. Takes more than a little skirmish with a few mangy cow thieves to knock me out of the saddle. Now I want you to take me home."

"Jess, I can't take you home till the doctor says so. And then you've got Joe and Johnny here to do that for you."

"No I don't. I fired them two."

"You told me while ago that you were payin' them."

"Well, I've fired them now. They won't take me home."

Webb smiled again. "I'm afraid you can't fire me, Jess. And I can't take you home."

Jess roared, "Dammit, if you're not goin' to help a man, git out of here!" Still smiling, Webb turned to go. He got as far as the next room when the cranky old rancher called to him, "Where do you think you're goin'? Come back here!"

"Got work to do, Jess."

"You sure do. You go catch them cow thieves before they git into my cattle again. If *I* catch them, I'll hang them."

"Better let *me* catch them, Jess."

"Then you get busy. I'll be back on my horse in a day or two, and I'll sure be a-lookin'."

Joe Vickers followed Webb to the door. They stood together in the darkness on the front porch. Webb asked, "He really gettin' along all right?"

"He's an old man, and an old man heals slow. He'll make

it all right, though, if we can keep him down long enough. Us old brushpoppers are hard to kill."

Webb turned to leave. Vickers said, "Webb . . ." The sheriff paused. "Webb, I still think it was Clabe Donovan I shot. Sure, I know what's happened, but I can still remember how things was. I don't nowise see how I could have made a mistake."

Webb made no reply.

"It ain't that I take any pride in killin' him, Webb; I don't. But I hate to see people gettin' themselves all nervous thinkin' he's back amongst them like a wolf in a flock of sheep. He's dead and gone; I'd stake my life on that."

"I never said different, Uncle Joe."

Walking back into his office, Webb lighted the lamp. The lamp chimney was still warm. He knew of no one else who would have had business here, so he figured it probably had been Sandy.

He glanced at Sandy's cot, expecting to see his brother's blanket roll and his warbag there where Sandy would have pitched them when he came in. They weren't. Some clothes that had been hanging on a nail weren't in sight either. Webb strode across and pulled out the top drawer of an old bureau they had used together. The drawer was empty. Sandy had taken everything he owned and had left.

"Hard-headed kid!" Webb breathed impatiently. "Won't listen and won't learn."

Webb leaned his shoulder against the steel bars of a cell and pondered what to do. He'd had his fight with Sandy, the only one he ever intended to have. He had said his piece and brought the boy in. He might go hunt him down again now and try to reason with him, but, if it came to the point of another fight, Webb wouldn't do it. A man could go only so far. Beyond that, it would be up to Sandy.

Quick footsteps pounded on the porch. Webb turned and saw Judge Upshaw stopping to lean heavily against the desk, shoulders a-heave with his hard breathing. The judge's face was flushed with excitement. He turned to look at Webb, and Webb could see the grip of fear in the man's eyes. Wordlessly the judge held up a piece of rope for Webb to see. He dropped into Webb's chair, his hands trembling.

Webb picked up the rope and felt a shock. It had been formed into a noose, with a hangman's knot.

"Where did you get it, judge?"

The judge was shaking so he could hardly answer. "Found it hanging on my door. I went down to the . . . went out on a legal matter. When I got back to the house I found this."

Webb fingered the knot thoughtfully. "Could be some kind of a joke."

"It doesn't look at all funny to me, sheriff. I want you to do something about it."

"First I'd have to have some idea who put it there."

The judge swallowed. "It was Clabe Donovan! It had to be him!"

"Judge, there's no use gettin' panicky. Frankly you've done some things here that have made some strong enemies for you. Could be one of them is usin' this Donovan talk to throw a scare into you."

"It's Donovan. I know it is. And he's going to kill me!"

Webb frowned and stared out the open door into the darkness. It made sense if Donovan *was* alive. The things the judge had said in the courtroom would have been enough to make Donovan hate him this much. It would have been like Clabe to want to make the judge eat his own words. Donovan was a man who could hate hard.

The judge said, "Webb, you've got to give me protection."

"How, Judge? The county budget only allows me one deputy, and he's placed way off in the upper end of the county."

"Send for him."

"Donovan swore to get revenge on lots of other people, too. I can't guard them all."

"I'm the county judge. You can certainly protect *me*."

"Bein' judge don't make your life worth more than anybody else's. If I had to tie myself to your apronstrings, I couldn't get out and hunt for Donovan."

"Webb, you've *got* to . . ."

It was then that Webb heard the shot. The blast echoed through town and stirred a dozen dogs into a frenzy of barking.

Judge Upshaw nearly fell out of his chair. For a second Webb thought the man was shot. Then he saw that the judge was gripped by panic.

Even before he heard a man begin calling for help, Webb sensed that the shot meant trouble. He was off the porch in two long strides and went running up the street. He saw people looking out of their doors. A few men began shouting. The shout was taken up quickly by others, both up and down the street.

"Where's the sheriff?" someone yelled. "Get Webb Matlock!"

Webb shouted, "Here I am. Where's the shootin' at?"

A cowboy appeared from between two buildings, pointing behind him. "Thisaway, Webb. Hurry." As Webb reached him, the cowboy turned and ran beside the sheriff, pointing the direction. "Over by Quince's corral. It's an awful thing, Webb, an awful thing."

Ahead of him, by the fence behind the livery barn, Webb could see men gathered, some of them gesturing excitedly, some standing in shocked silence. Webb pushed his way through. "Let me in there, boys."

Someone held a lantern. On the ground lay a man. As the lantern holder extended his arm, bringing the light over the body, Webb felt a chill run through him. Involuntarily he turned away.

"Uncle Joe Vickers, isn't it?" he asked tightly.

Quince Pyburn stood with his shoulders slumped. "Not much left to go by, but it's him, Webb. Caught a shotgun blast full in the face."

Webb made himself look again. A sickness welled up inside him. Over by the corral he could hear a man retching. In the pale glow of the lantern he recognized Johnny Willet. "What happened?" Webb asked Quince.

The liveryman shook his head. "Can't rightly say. Johnny was there. He saw it, but he's been shook too bad to talk."

The men stepped aside so Webb could walk over to Johnny and put his hand on the cowboy's shoulder. "How about it, Johnny? What can you tell us?"

Johnny turned, his body trembling a little, his face paled

from shock. "Webb, it was . . ." His voice broke. He looked down a moment, clenching his fists in an effort to regain strength. "We was on our way to sleep in Quince's wagon-yard. We got right here when a man suddenly rose up over yonder." Johnny pointed off into the darkness. "He wasn't more than twelve, fifteen feet away. He says to Joe, he says, 'Is that Joe Vickers?' Joe stops and says, 'Yeah, I'm him. Who are you?' Without a word, this feller raises up a shotgun and lets Joe have a full blast. Joe never knew what hit him. Me, I was petrified. I just stood there waitin' for him to kill me too. Then this feller says to me, he says, 'Tell the rest of them around here that Clabe Donovan owes a lot of debts, and they're all goin' to be paid.' "

Johnny shuddered and looked down at the old ranch fore-man who had so long been his friend.

Webb could feel cold sweat. It had to be true, then. To question the fact any longer was idle. Clabe Donovan was alive and seeking vengeance!

Joe Vickers had said he would stake his life on the fact that he had killed Clabe Donovan. And Joe Vickers was dead.

Webb said, "Johnny, which way did Clabe go after the shootin'?"

Johnny frowned, trying to remember. He rubbed his hand against his cheek. "I think he had a horse tied back around at that corral. I remember hearin' some horses go off in a lope."

Quince Pyburn said, "I expect he's right, Webb. I was the first one here. I heard the shot and came runnin'. I heard horses headin' east."

Someone shouted, "Let's go get him!" Some of the crowd surged away.

Webb yelled, "Hold on, boys. No use goin' off out there now."

Men protested. Webb held up his hand for silence. "Boys, you couldn't find him in that dark. Go ridin' off now and all you'll do is mess up his tracks so nobody can trail him."

Johnny Willet was getting his composure back. "What're you goin' to do, just let him get flat away?"

Soberly Webb said, "It may be the hardest job we ever did, but we've got to make ourselves wait till daylight. Then we'll track him. He'll have a long start, but he's got to stop someplace and rest. Once we start, we don't stop. We'll stay on his trail till we've got him run back to his hole. We'll get him."

The men talked it over among themselves and grudgingly admitted that this was the only course which really made sense. Johnny Willet said grimly, "Just tell us what time to meet you, Webb. You'll have a-plenty of help."

Webb nodded, satisfied. "Right here at Quince's barn. We'll ride at the first light. Everybody bring along enough food to last him a couple or three days. Now go get yourselves a good night's sleep, because you may not get much more rest for a while."

The men scattered into the night, talking quietly among themselves. In the cold gray of dawn some of them would change their minds about going. But Webb knew he would have enough men for the job.

Quince Pyburn said, "No use goin' after the doctor for Uncle Joe. Guess he needs the undertaker instead."

Webb nodded. "Go get him, will you, Quince?" Then to Johnny Willet he said, "We better go break this to Jess Leggett."

Old Jess sat in grieving silence. Johnny Willet stood looking out into the darkness while Webb told about it. "Clabe must have found out that Uncle Joe had been sleepin' in the wagonyard the last couple or three nights, and he knew to wait for him there."

Eyes glazing, Jess blew his nose. "Why Joe? Why not me or any one of a dozen others? The time we tried and convicted Clabe, he swore he'd get loose and pay off a lot of us—you because you was the sheriff; Florentino Rodriguez because he tracked Clabe down; me because it was mostly me and my men who hounded Clabe to the end; the judge and the jury because they condemned him to hang. How come he picked Joe to start on?"

Webb sat with his hands clasped tightly together, his grief a dull ache because he had regarded Uncle Joe Vickers almost as blood kin. "Man on the dodge can't always be figured out, Jess. He does crazy things sometimes. For years now, everybody has thought Clabe Donovan was dead. Joe Vickers got the credit for killin' him, blastin' him off his horse with both barrels of a shotgun. When Clabe decided to show he was still alive, maybe he thought it would be appropriate to kill the man who was supposed to have killed *him*, and do it the same way Uncle Joe was supposed to have done."

"Sounds crazy to me."

"Maybe Clabe *is* crazy now, Jess. That makes him all the more dangerous. It's all the more reason we got to get him!"

Webb knocked on the door of the little frame house where Ellie Donovan lived. He could see a lamp burning inside. He saw her shadow fall across the curtain that covered the oval glass in the door. Then she stood framed against the lamplight.

Webb said apologetically, "Ellie, I know I told you I wouldn't come to your house anymore, but this time I had to. I . . ." He broke off to stare at her. "You look like you'd seen a ghost. What's the matter, Ellie?"

She stepped back into the room, and he followed her. She said in a trembling voice, "That shot . . . it had something to do with Clabe, didn't it?"

He nodded. "Yes, Ellie, it did. How did you know?"

"He was here."

"You saw him? You talked to him?"

She shook her head. "I was sitting here sewing a dress. All of a sudden I got the feeling someone was watching me. I went to the window and looked out. That's when I saw him, standing in the shadows. I ran to the front door and called to him, but he was gone."

"You're sure it was Clabe?"

"I didn't see him close, but I could make out the Mexican hat, and I could recognize the way Clabe had of standing. I could feel his presence, Webb. Somehow, even before I saw him, I sensed that it was Clabe, and he was watching me."

Webb stood with his hands shoved deep into his pockets. "That was before you heard the shot?"

"A little while."

Webb bit his lip. It all added up. He told Ellie about Joe Vickers. She listened incredulously. "He was bad in lots of ways, Webb, but it wasn't like him to stand there and kill a man that way."

"He did though, Ellie. He's changed." He stared at her in a swelling of sympathy, wanting to take her in his arms but knowing now that he couldn't. He could never do it again so long as Clabe Donovan lived. "Ellie, we're goin' after him in the mornin'. One way or another, we've got to stop him. If it comes to that, we might even have to . . ." He frowned. "It may be me who has to fire the shot."

She buried her face in her hands.

Webb said, "I hope you won't hate me, Ellie."

She didn't reply. He waited a moment, hoping she might. Then knowing she wouldn't, he turned and left the house.

He crossed into the Mexican settlement afoot and moved down a dark, dusty street. Lanterns glowed in front of cantinas, and lamplight shone from the sometimes-glassless windows of adobe houses. Not recognizing him as the sheriff, a woman in a shadowy doorway spoke softly to him in Spanish, and he ignored her. A happy Mexican song drifted to him on the cool night breeze, its verses lusty and ribald.

Webb walked around a small adobe general store to the living quarters in the rear. The door was wide open, and Webb could see most of the inside. But it would be impolite to enter or even to look in without first announcing himself. He called, "Florentino!"

A man got up from a rawhide chair and limped to the door. *"Si?"* Squinting into the darkness, he smiled as recognition came. "Mister Webb." He motioned with his hand. *"Pase, pase."* Florentino was still a young man, not past thirty.

Webb took off his hat and bent a little to enter the low door. A Mexican woman sat in an oversized old rocking chair. She arose, and Webb saw that she was heavy with child. "*Señor* sheriff, please to sit down."

A young man stood up from a bench in the corner. This was Aparicio Rodriguez, Florentino's cousin.

Florentino and Aparicio had worked on the ranches. They could speak and understand English well enough, but Florentino's wife had only meager knowledge of the language. Webb shifted to Spanish, which he could handle with fair ease if not with accuracy. "Please, Consuela, keep your chair. I'll sit on this bench." A little girl, a yearling-past, sat on the bare dirt floor, looking up suspiciously at Webb. He knelt and stuck out his hand as if to pinch the girl's chin. The baby backed away from him. But she didn't back far. It wouldn't take her long to warm up, Webb thought. If he had a lump or two of that brown *piloncillo* sugar from Mexico . . .

By the look of Consuela Rodriguez, Webb knew it wouldn't be many days before the little *muchacha* had a new brother or sister to share the adobe house with. She was a handsome woman, this Consuela, but like most of her people in that time, she faced a life of hard work and privation. Already it had begun to show on her. By the time she was thirty she would look forty. When she was forty, she would look old.

Webb said, "I came to ask a favor of you, Florentino. Whether you choose to do it or not is up to you, and you alone. Because of your family . . ." he glanced at the woman and the child ". . . you may want to think about it a little."

He told what had happened tonight, and about his plan to take out a posse in the morning. "Florentino, you're the best tracker in the county. There's not a *gringo* can touch you. Without you, we might find Donovan and we might not. With you, I think we could track him clear to Mexico City. But there's a hazard: the tracker is always the one out front, the one easiest to kill. That's why you'll have to make up your own mind. I won't try to pressure you."

Florentino frowned darkly, studying his little family a long time. "I have heard the talk about Clabe Donovan, but I thought it was only talk." Mouth tightening, he said, "He spoke of old debts, did he?"

Webb repeated what Johnny Willet had said.

Rodriguez recalled, "Never will I forget what he promised when I tracked him and led you to where he was hiding. He shot me in the leg, remember? After he was caught, he called me a greaser, this Clabe Donovan. He looked at me as if he could kill me with his eyes. He said, 'You dirty Mex, someday I'll get you. Next time I'll kill you so dead that even the buzzards will leave you alone!' "

Webb nodded. "I remember. He threatened a lot of people. But he's gone all these years without carrying out any of the threats."

Florentino said pointedly, "He has begun now."

The Mexican slowly walked back and forth across the small, lime-plastered room, thinking. One leg was board-stiff because of Donovan's bullet. Walking was not easy for him. He stopped and looked again at his family. "Mister Joe was a good friend of mine. I worked a long time for him and Mister Jess. When my leg was ruined, they helped me buy the store so I would have a way to live. They came when Consuela and I were married. My boy's name is going to be José, for Mister Joe." Florentino turned, saddened. "Another time, I would gladly help you find the man who killed him. But any day now, Consuela's time will come. I cannot be away when my first son is born."

Webb was disappointed, but he felt no blame for Florentino. "I know how it is. Thanks, anyway." He turned toward the door.

Young Aparicio spoke quickly, "Wait, Master Webb. I have no baby coming. I can go."

Webb said, "You are not Florentino."

"I am his cousin, and Florentino has taught me how to track. No man can do it better, except Florentino."

Webb saw concern in Florentino's eyes, worry for Aparicio. Family ties were strong among Mexican people. Florentino said, "He is good, Mister Webb. But he is also young and a little headstrong."

Webb could see Aparicio's eagerness. "You'd have to take

orders, Aparicio. You'd have to do whatever I say, or I'd send you home."

The young man said quickly, "Anything you say, I will do. Mister Joe was good to me. I want to help find the man who killed him."

Not sure, Webb hesitated. But he knew he needed the youth. Webb was no tracker for a job like this. He didn't know a *gringo* in Dry Fork who was.

Finally he nodded. "All right. Daylight, then. I'll send a man with a horse."

The lamp was burning in Webb's office when he returned. He walked in with a sense of relief, expecting to find Sandy. Instead he saw Birdie Hanks, sitting in the chair by the roll-top desk. She arose.

"Birdie," he said, surprised. "I sure didn't expect to find you here."

"Sandy's gone," she blurted. Looking closer, Webb could tell she had been crying.

"Gone where?"

She shook her head. "I don't know. Did he leave any word here for you?"

"No, all he did was gather his gear and ride off while I was out of the office. Took everything he owned."

Near crying again, the girl said, "It was the fight that capped it, I suppose. He said he had argued with you lots of times, but you'd never actually fought before."

Soberly Webb said, "It wasn't my choice. I didn't want to."

"Sandy told me he was on his way out. Told me he was going to live his own life and let you be shed of him. Said he'd be back to see me someday. Then he kissed me goodbye and rode off."

"Didn't even tell you whichaway he was headed?"

"Not a word."

Back out to Bronc Tomlin's I'll bet, Webb thought angrily.

He took a handkerchief and touched it to a tear rolling down Birdie's cheek. "Don't you go cryin' over him. He's young and so are you. He'll get to thinkin' about you, and he won't be able to stay away. You watch, he'll be back."

"You really think so?"

"Bet you anything."

She tried to force a smile. "He's a hard man to put up with sometimes. But I guess I couldn't forget him if I tried."

"Have patience, Birdie. He'll come back."

The girl left. Webb's smile left with her. Soberly he blew out the lamp, undressed, and flopped down on his cot. He lay there a long time, unable to sleep. In his mind he kept seeing Ellie Donovan and Clabe Donovan and Uncle Joe Vickers. Most of all, he kept seeing Sandy Matlock.

He knew he didn't really believe what he had told Birdie. Maybe this time Sandy wouldn't come back.

5

ARRIVING AT THE LIVERY BARN WELL BEFORE DAYLIGHT, Webb found Quince Pyburn feeding the horses. Quince already had one saddled for himself. The liveryman said, "I got Juan Obregon comin' over directly to take care of the place for me. I'm goin' with you."

"You don't have to, Quince."

"I knew Joe Vickers a long time. Wasn't no squarer man ever walked the streets of this town. Thinkin' of myself, too. I was foreman of the jury that convicted Clabe Donovan. I'd rather be lookin' for him than have him lookin' for me."

Webb nodded approval. "I don't know anybody I'd rather have ride with me, Quince. Come along, and welcome."

One by one the other men began gathering. Webb picked a horse for Aparicio Rodriguez and had a rider lead the animal across the town, bareback. Aparicio would have his own saddle. Before long the puncher returned, the young tracker beside him. Rodriguez rode a big-horned Mexico saddle but wore a plain Texas-style cowboy hat instead of a wide-brimmed Mexican sombrero. Good judgment, Webb reflected. With Donovan wearing a sombrero, and with men being excitable the way they were in the confusion of a gunfight, somebody might make a mistake.

"How is Florentino's wife this mornin'?" Webb asked.

"Consuela, she is having the pains. Pretty soon now is

time, she say. But for that, I think Florentino make me stay home and he go instead."

Webb nodded. He had rather have had it that way. Aparicio was still an unknown quantity. Likely the boy would prove to be as good as Florentino had said. But Webb liked to play the safe game when he could.

Johnny Willet showed up, dark-eyed and grim. It was evident he hadn't slept. Webb said, "Don't you want to stay for the funeral, Johnny? They'll be buryin' Uncle Joe today."

Johnny shook his head. "I'd rather bury the man who killed him."

The eastern sky began to glow pink. First daylight crept across the prairie. Webb glanced at Aparicio. "Reckon it's light enough to commence followin' tracks?"

Rodriguez nodded with the confidence of youth. "You bet."

Judge Upshaw came hurrying from the direction of his house, greatly disturbed. He was breathing hard when he stopped by Webb's horse. "Sheriff, what do you mean, taking all of these men?"

"We're goin' after Clabe Donovan."

"But those of us in town need protection. Who are you leaving here to make sure Donovan doesn't come back and kill us all?"

Evenly Webb said, "The only way to get Clabe Donovan is to go where he's at, not wait for him to come and pick us off one by one."

Upshaw was trembling. "But what if you miss him? He could come back and kill me. You know he said he would."

Badly as he disliked the judge, Webb felt a momentary pity for the man. "You can go with us if you'd like to."

The judge stepped back. "I . . . I have court business here."

Webb nodded. "Well, then, good luck." He motioned to Aparicio. "Let's be gettin' at it."

The judge called after him, "Matlock . . ." Then Upshaw gave up. He turned his back and started hurrying toward his house.

Quince Pyburn remarked, "Did you see that gun he's got shoved into his waistband? Liable to kill somebody with it."

A cowboy said, "I walked by his house last night. He was hangin' blankets up over the windows so nobody could see in. I expect he's bolted the doors."

Quince said, "God help the first poor Mexican who steps up onto that porch. Judge is liable to shoot anything that wears a sombrero."

The possemen held back while Aparicio examined the sign around back of Quince's corral. The Mexican looked a minute or so and gave his verdict:

"Four men here. Three stay with the horses while one, he goes afoot to the corner of the corral. This one, I think, is Clabe Donovan. After he is shoot Mister Joe, he run back to the horses. All four men, they ride away."

Webb never had claimed to know a lot about tracks, but it seemed to be as Aparicio said. He could see the stubs of cigarettes lying around where the three men had waited. He turned in the saddle. "Boys, we'll stay off to one side of the tracks. Aparicio will be the only one who rides in close. Time comes we have to check back on them, we don't want them rubbed out."

Rodriguez took the lead eagerly, like a young hound turned loose on a scent. The posse strung out behind him and a little to the left, moving in an easy trot. It was not a difficult trail to follow. It had been made in darkness, with little chance for cover-up. With daylight, Donovan might start hiding his trail. Then would come Aparicio's real test.

For a while the tracks led the posse east. A thought began needling Webb. After upwards of an hour he called a halt, signaled the Mexican back and waited for the men to circle in around him.

"Boys, I think they're headin' east to lead us astray. Ten to one, Clabe figures sooner or later to strike south for the Rio Grande. Likely he'll go east till he gets to a creek or a gravel bed where he can lose his tracks. Then he'll cut south, countin' on us to waste a lot of time tryin' to pick up his trail somewhere to the east. Looks to me like we can gain time if we drop south now, bearin' east a mite. If I'm right, we'll eventually cross his trail. Short-cuttin' him, we could gain some hours. And we sure do need them."

If I'm right? And if I'm wrong ...

Webb could simply have made it in the form of a command, but he wanted the men's approval. He was no army officer, expecting blind obedience, and these were not soldiers to give it. He saw no sign of argument.

Quince Pyburn said, "It's a gamble, Webb. But then, what in life ain't a gamble? Lead the way."

Gratified, Webb nodded. "We'll fan out and watch the ground. Can't afford to miss those tracks when we cross over them."

They rode in a steady trot, Webb occasionally giving his horse a gentle touch of the spurs, putting him into an easy lope for short stretches to gain on Donovan. Daylight broke full across the land, and the sun began its climb in a sky from which the thin morning clouds slowly dissolved. By midmorning the sky was clear and the sun already hot. Though impatience prickled him, Webb no longer allowed himself the time-gaining runs in which he had indulged during the cool hours of early morning. Now the horses had to be held in, had to be spared.

There had been no sign of tracks leading south. A couple of times the riders crossed suspicious trails, but Aparicio pronounced them to have been left by loose horses, meandering in the devious patterns which grazing animals make.

As noon came on, Webb's face lengthened with worry. It had been a risk, striking south instead of staying with Donovan's actual tracks, but it had seemed a reasonable gamble. Now Webb began to suffer doubt. What if Donovan hadn't gone south? What if he had intended all along to go east? Worse, what if he had doubled back? Clabe Donovan had always possessed a fox's cunning. He might purposely have led the pursuit astray so he could slip back into town.

Joe Vickers might have been only the beginning.

It seemed to Webb that they should have come across the southbound tracks by now if there were any. The specter of failure rode on Webb's shoulder, but he didn't turn back. He had made his decision and would stick with it. Too late to stop Donovan now if the man *had* outwitted him. Webb could only go on with his plan as he had started it, gambling all the chips on one card.

Aparicio still rode out front, his dark brown eyes intently studying the ground. Watching him, Webb had come to feel confident the youth wouldn't miss much. Young, maybe, but in his veins flowed the same blood as Florentino's.

The sun was about noon high when Rodriguez reined up suddenly. He lifted his hand, and the other riders stopped. Aparicio swung to the ground, legs stiff from the long ride. He knelt and fingered a set of tracks. When he stood up, his white teeth were shining.

"You call him right, Mister Webb. These are the ones, the same four." He pointed. "South they go, straight like a shot."

Relief lifted Webb's shoulders. Without meaning to, he let his mouth crack open in a broad grin. He breathed a long sigh as he looked back at the men behind him and saw them perk up. Doubtless the same worry had nagged them all. Probably they knew how it had plagued him, but they hadn't said a word to add to his own self-doubt.

"Aparicio, can you tell how old the tracks are?"

The Mexican pointed his chin downtrail. "From the sign, I say this trail she is not very old. Two, three hours. Maybeso these men think they are safe, and they stop to sleep a little in the night. We have make a pretty good gain, looks like."

Quince Pyburn eyed Webb Matlock with appreciation. "Man who don't ever gamble nothin' don't ever win nothin'. But it had me boogered a while, Webb."

Webb said, "We better stop and eat us a bite; let the horses blow a little."

The men ate hurriedly from the food they had brought along. Finished, they swung into their saddles and rode again. Excitement began to build in Webb. He fought down a strong impulse to run the horses awhile, to try catching up faster. The sun was hot. Sweat was beginning to stick the shirt to his back. He could sense that the horse was tiring beneath him. A man could expect only so much from an animal.

They had ridden into the rough country that was Bronc Tomlin's Rafter T land. Ahead, Webb saw a scattering of trees. Aparicio, up front, reined in and looked at the ground. Webb touched spurs to his horse and caught up to the tracker.

"Here," Rodriguez pointed to the ground, "they change horses. See where ropes rub on the trunks of those trees? They stake horses here yesterday and leave them. While ago they come by, saddle those horses and turn the others loose."

Webb studied the sign. From the close-cropped grass and the droppings, it was easy to tell that four horses had been staked here a long time.

Aparicio said, "Donovan, he is ride south again. And on fresh horses. The loose horses, they drift off yonderway."

Gritting his teeth, Webb glanced back at the possemen who had caught up and gathered around him. "Bronc Tomlin's headquarters. Donovan used Rafter T horses, I'd bet my bottom dollar."

Quince Pyburn swore. "We ought to bring Bronc out here and stretch his neck from one of these here trees."

Webb said, "That'd make us as bad as he is. There's somethin' we can do, though. We'll go down there and make Bronc lend us some fresh horses."

Quince clenched his fist. "I hope he says no."

"He won't. He'll act surprised that Donovan used his horses, and he'll say he's real glad to be of help to us."

Riding toward the ranchhouse, they came upon the four horses the outlaws had ridden. The animals were slowly drifting in the direction of water, grazing as they went. Sweat had dried on their hides, and not long ago.

Bronc Tomlin walked out from his corrals to meet the possemen, his hand up in a thin semblance of friendliness. "Howdy, fellers. Git down and we'll fix us some coffee." He looked innocently at Webb Matlock. "Never figured to see you so soon after the last time, sheriff. You huntin' that brother of yours?"

The way the man said it gave Webb a start. "Is he here?"

"Any reason he ought to be?"

That was no answer. Webb frowned, his teeth digging into his lower lip. He hadn't had much time today to let his mind dwell on Sandy. Now he would have to admit there was a good chance the boy had come back out here last night.

Angry as Sandy had been, it would be a logical way for him to show his defiance. "You didn't answer my question, Bronc."

The rancher smiled dryly, showing brown-stained teeth. "You're welcome to look around."

Webb glared at Tomlin a moment, then switched the subject. "Bronc, we came to borrow some fresh horses."

Bronc was on the point of putting up an argument. "Now, sheriff . . ."

"Before you say another word, listen! Clabe Donovan did a murder last night in Dry Fork. He and three others got away on Rafter T horses. There's a lot of folks believe you let them have them, and they'll be real put out if you act like you don't want us to catch up with him."

Tomlin's gaze flicked from one man to another, and he seemed to sense their hair-trigger temper. He began to backtrack. "Sheriff, I wasn't goin' to say you couldn't have no horses. Sure, you just help yourself to anything you want. I'll do anything I can."

Webb suggested blandly, "You could go along and help us."

Tomlin quickly shook his shaggy head. "I would, only I got some broncs here that I couldn't just ride off and leave."

The possemen quickly changed horses. Starting out fresh, Quince Pyburn looked darkly back over his thin shoulder. "I still say we ought to stretch his neck a foot or two."

"We can't prove anything on him," Webb said. "Just give him plenty of rope. Someday he'll strangle on it."

Rather than go back where Donovan and his men had changed horses, the posse cut south, angling just enough to intercept the Donovan trail farther down. Eventually they found it. With the fresh horses, Webb no longer feared to spur into a lope.

"We still got distance to close up," he said, "and it's not far to the river."

From sign, they could tell they were gaining. Evidently feeling sure of himself, Donovan had slowed down. But Webb could soon see that even with this advantage, the posse wouldn't catch up before it reached the river. Donovan had beaten them there.

At last Aparicio rode through the thick maze of green brush that screened the edge of the stream. He stopped his horse on the silty bank of the muddy, slow-moving Rio Grande. He didn't have to point down at the tracks in the mud. They were plain for all to see. Squinting, Webb could see where the tracks came out on the other side of the river. Even from here, he could tell they were still fairly wet. Probably not an hour old.

Webb glanced around at Quince and the others. "Well, boys," he said, "here we are. Wouldn't surprise me if Clabe's across yonder in the brush, snickerin' at us."

Quince Pyburn swore, a task at which he was proficient. Johnny Willet said grimly, "Ain't nothin' but just another river. I've swum many a river on the trail to Kansas."

Webb fingered the badge on his shirt. "Not like this one. Across yonder is a different county, a different law. This badge don't mean much when we cross over."

Johnny said, "But you got a .44 on your hip and a saddlegun under your leg. They means a-plenty no matter where they're at."

Webb glanced at Aparicio. "You game to go across?"

"Ready when you say."

Webb drew the saddlegun and held it in his right hand to keep it from getting wet. "All right, let's see if these Bronc Tomlin horses can swim."

It was the dry season of year, and the river was running low. The horses had little trouble because their feet were on the soft bottom most of the way across. The only mishap came when Johnny Willet's horse lost its footing and plunged the cowboy into the river. The other men moved in quickly to help. Shifting the rifle to his left hand, Webb grabbed Johnny beneath one arm and pulled the cowboy up against his saddle. Johnny sputtered but held on until they got across the river. On the far bank he dropped to his knees and coughed up some of the muddy water.

Concerned, Webb asked, 'You goin' to make it all right, Johnny?"

Johnny blinked away the eye-burning river sand. "All right. Just didn't figure on a bath, is all."

Someone brought Johnny's horse. The cowboy swung up, his clothes dripping. He said, "Let's don't be losin' no time on my account."

Webb started to lead out but pulled up when he heard Quince Pyburn grunt, "Uh oh, we got company comin'." Webb turned his horse and saw soldiers riding along the edge of the river, moving up on them in an easy lope.

What a time, he thought, to run into the Mexican cavalry?

There were upwards of a dozen soldiers mounted on scrubby little Mexican ponies that had never seen enough feed a day in their lives. The lieutenant was easy to spot, not only because he rode out front but also because he had the only good horse in the bunch. It was a handsome sorrel that stood two hands taller than any other animal in the lot.

The sand finally blinked away, Johnny Willet remarked, "I know that sorrel horse. He's old Jess Leggett's Big Red, stole a couple of months ago by some horse thieves from this side of the river."

Webb knew how it was with these isolated Mexican border detachments, serving under only a modicum of real military law. Each officer ran things pretty much to suit himself, sometimes taking bribes or receiving stolen property in return for protection to those who preyed on the rest of the Mexican populace, or on the *gringos* across the river. Some of these officers demanded tribute from the poor people they were supposed to be protecting. Sometimes they falsified purchases and charged up artificially high prices to their government while they lined their own pockets. Under little supervision, corrupt officers could rule as virtual dictators within their own areas of command, holding even the power of life and death.

An ugly picture, but who was to tell? It was a long way to Mexico City.

The lieutenant halted his patrol. On command, the soldiers fanned out on either side of him, as if they meant business.

To Webb they looked like mercenaries of the worst kind, dregs of the border towns, their faces tough, their eyes brutal. The officer looked grimly over the Texas posse, seeking the man in charge. He spotted Webb's badge, and his cold dark eyes lifted to Webb's face. In passable English he said, "You have come to invade Mexico? Your army is small."

Webb had met some Mexican officers he liked and some he disliked. He had classified this one on sight. "We're on the trail of some outlaws who crossed the river ahead of us."

"I see no outlaws."

Webb pointed. "That there's their tracks."

The officer didn't look. "I see no tracks."

Then Webb knew. The lieutenant was in league with Donovan.

The officer's gaze roved once more over the possemen and settled on Aparicio Rodriguez. Resentment coloring his voice, he said in Spanish, "What sort of Mexican are you, riding with these *gringos?*"

"The outlaws we seek are not Mexican, they are *gringo*. They killed a man."

"A *gringo?*" the lieutenant asked. When Aparicio nodded, the man said, "What we need, then, are more *gringo* outlaws. Let the *gringos* kill off each other." His eyes narrowed as he studied the young tracker. "If you lived on this side of the river, I would teach you a lesson about riding with these men. You are a traitor to your own kind!"

The quick temper of youth flared in Aparicio. "And you are a dog, to wear the uniform and be in league with killers. You are worse than they are because they claim to be nothing else. You are supposed to be a soldier."

Anger leaped in the lieutenant's eyes. "Careful. On this side of the river I am the master. When I speak, everyone jumps."

Aparicio stiffened. "I am not jumping. I say you are a dog!"

The lieutenant's arm streaked, and a sword flashed into his hand. "You are only a *peon*. No *peon* speaks to me that way." For a second it appeared he would drive the sword into the boy. But he caught himself and lowered the blade.

Fire crackled in his eyes. "Go back, *peon*, and stay. If I ever catch you on this side again . . ."

The officer's gaze cut back to Webb. He reverted to English. "You go now, back *al otro lado*." His voice was sharp with command.

Sullenly Webb said, "We came to get those outlaws."

The lieutenant waved the sword point at Webb. "You are here against Mexican law. By right we could shoot you, all of you. But the heart of Tiburcio Armendariz is kind. We let you go, *this time!*"

"You're protectin' murderers and you know it."

"You go to Mexico City, *gringo*. Get papers from *el presidente*. Then perhaps Armendariz lets you look for your outlaws. Now go!"

Face flushed, Webb clenched his fists in helpless anger. He muttered under his breath to the men around him. "They got us dead to rights."

Johnny Willet said stubbornly, "Between us we could whip the whole bunch."

Quince Pyburn replied, "And start a sure-enough border war? Webb's right, we got no legal status here. If we hadn't got caught, fine. But we did get caught, and we better get ourselves back across the *rio*."

Webb reined his horse toward the water, frustration boiling in him. Johnny Willet hung back. "We could take them, I know we could."

"Come on, Johnny," said Webb.

The lieutenant hailed Webb, halting him at the river's edge. "*Gringo!* We watch this river. You try to come back, we shoot you before you are out of the water!"

They swam across to the Texas side. Looking over his shoulder, Webb could see the patrol remained where it was, watching them. He swung down. "We best let the horses blow a spell." His trousers were soaked, his toes squishing in water-filled boots.

All eyes watched the Mexican soldiers. Webb could sense the men's simmering anger.

Johnny Willet felt his shirt pocket, then said thinly,

"Webb, you got the makin's? All my tobacco was soaked when I took that fall."

Webb handed him a sack of tobacco. Johnny rolled himself a smoke while his angry eyes fastened on the distant patrol. "You ain't aimin' to let the thing lie the way it is, are you?"

"We did the best we could, Johnny. We couldn't have known there'd be a patrol to stop us the minute we got across."

"We could ride up or down the river a ways and try again."

"They'd pick up our tracks and come a-huntin' us. I'd hate to have the thing come to a shoot-out because in the eyes of the law we'd be in the wrong. Across yonder we're trespassers."

"That Armendariz has got some kind of agreement with Clabe Donovan," Johnny said bitterly.

"Sure he has. But you'd have to go all the way to Mexico City to get anything done about it."

Johnny Willet leaned against his dripping horse and stared across the saddle at the men on the far bank of the Rio Grande. "I intend to do somethin' about it. One way or another, old Joe Vickers is goin' to have the account settled for him."

"We'll do somethin', Johnny," Webb promised. "But I don't reckon it'll be today."

"There's too many of us," Johnny agreed. "One or two might be able to slip across there and make it."

"Forget it, Johnny."

But Johnny didn't forget it. They camped for the night a couple of miles north of the river to rest and dry out. At daylight Webb was awakened by distant gunfire. Jumping to his feet, he found that Johnny Willet and Aparicio Rodriguez had gone. Their tracks led south.

Webb and the others saddled quickly and spurred toward the river, following the plain tracks. At the bank they pulled up in dismay.

On the near edge, Johnny Willet sat hunched in the mud,

breathing hard from exhaustion. His right hand gripped his left shoulder, and crimson edged slowly out between his fingers. Aparicio lay crumpled where Johnny had dragged him out of the river. A dark red stain drained off into the water. Without touching him, Webb knew the young Mexican was dead.

Looking across the river in helpless fury, Webb could see the Mexican patrol, guns in their hands, the lieutenant in the center of the soldiers. Webb also saw someone else: a broad-shouldered man wearing *gringo* clothes and a black Mexican sombrero. Even from here, he knew that shape, that stance.

Donovan!

6

ONE OF THE POSSEMEN FIRED A VENGEFUL SHOT IN THE direction of the Mexican patrol, but it didn't hit anybody.

"No more shootin'!" Webb ordered sharply.

With Quince Pyburn's help he picked up Johnny Willet and half-dragged him back into the brush beyond the river bank. Someone else brought the young Mexican's body and carefully laid it out in the shade of a mesquite. Shade would help the boy none now, but it still seemed the thing to do.

Webb tore Johnny's sleeve for a look at the wound. Johnny protested weakly. "I'm all right, it's just a scratch. How about Aparicio?"

"Dead."

Johnny's head drooped. "I thought he was. Couldn't tell for sure. So winded there wasn't much I could do after I drug him out of the water."

Webb knew he should reproach the cowboy, but it would serve no useful purpose now. The harm was done. The stricken look in Johnny's eyes showed that nothing Webb could say would hurt half as much as what had already happened.

"It was a stupid thing to try," Johnny spoke tightly. "It was my idea. Thought the two of us could get somethin' done, him trackin', me along for an extra gun. We never got halfway across the river. They must have seen us the minute we came out of the brush. But they laid back and waited. They let us get way into the water before they came out and opened up. The man in the sombrero—Donovan, I guess it was—shot the horse out from under me. That Lieutenant Armendariz, he was the one that got Aparicio. Hit him in the shoulder first, knocked him out of the saddle. Boy was cryin' and chokin'. Armendariz just kept on shootin', puttin' bullets into him. Seemed like it pleasured him to do it."

Webb examined Johnny's wound. "Deep gash, but clean. Bullet went on through. It'll get sore as sin, but it'll heal. Quince, I brought a bottle of whisky along for a case like this. It's in my saddlebag."

Quince said, "I'll get it."

Johnny didn't seem to care about himself. "He was a game little Mex, that Aparicio, game as ever I seen."

Webb said, "It's done now. Won't help to cry over what's already done."

Johnny's teeth clenched as Webb poured a little of the whisky over the wound. "Webb, I took him into that scrape. It was my fault. I'm goin' to see to it that he didn't die for nothin'."

With a stirring of impatience Webb asked, "Don't you think you've done enough already?"

"I ain't even started!"

"You've started and you've finished. You're goin' home, Johnny."

Johnny shook his head. "I've dealt myself into this game to stay. I'll play it out to the last hand."

Webb sat on his spurred heels, wrapping a cloth around the cowboy's wound and studying Johnny's face. He saw a stolid determination there and knew argument was useless. "What do you think you could do?"

"I'll think of somethin'."

"You can't go back across that river. None of us are goin' to, at least not yet awhile."

Johnny nodded grimly. "I know. I learned my lesson there. But there's bound to be another way." He sat a while, sorrowfully staring at the body of the young Mexican. "Florentino's goin' to take it hard, Webb. They were as close as brothers, him and Aparicio. If it hadn't been for me . . ."

"Don't keep beatin' yourself over the head, Johnny. Maybe it *was* your idea, but he went of his own will, same as you did."

Johnny pushed onto his feet, wincing a little and gripping his burning shoulder. He glanced from one to another of the men scattered around him as if he were looking for some sign of blame. He found none. At length he turned back to the sheriff. "Webb, you ain't got a deputy, have you? I mean, a full-time deputy in Dry Fork?"

Webb shook his head. "Been several years since the county needed one."

"You need one now. And I'm it."

"Johnny, you've got a good job with Jess Leggett."

"I got a bigger job to do right now."

Webb knew a moment of exasperation, but he also knew by looking at the cowboy that argument would be wasted on him. "Takes more than just wantin' the job to make a man a deputy."

"I'll do the job, Webb, whether you hire me or not. So you'd just as well put me on the payroll and make it legal."

"What about Jess?"

"He's got enough help to take care of his cows."

"Have you figured out just what you could do, Johnny?"

Johnny's jaw was set firm. "It's a long ways to Dry Fork, Webb. You got to stay around there most of the time. You can't be down here a-ridin' this river. But somebody needs to." He frowned. "Way I see it, Donovan has got to cross the *rio* before he can make a raid on anybody. He can't cross without leavin' tracks.

"This is a long old river, but Donovan always did it in the same general area, every time. Now, supposin' I was to stay here and do nothin' but ride that river up and down, day in and day out. Unless he goes a long ways upstream or down, Donovan can't cross without me either seein' him or cuttin' his sign in a matter of hours. With a fast horse, and knowin' whichaway he's headed, I got a good chance of beatin' him there."

Webb rubbed his chin, uncertain. "Johnny . . ."

"I'm goin' to do it whether I got a badge or not, and whether you pay me or not. I'd just a little rather you made it legal, is all."

Webb gave in, knowing he had just as well. "Then I'll make it legal, Johnny."

Webb didn't want to ride down the main street, leading Aparicio's horse with the young Mexican's tarp-wrapped body tied across it and getting the town all stirred up. He circled Dry Fork, entering by way of the Mexican settlement. He was dusty and bearded and felt as badly as he looked. He reined up in front of the small adobe store run by Florentino Rodriguez. He glanced back at weary, slump-shouldered Quince Pyburn as if to ask him for support. But this was a job that wouldn't improve, even with help.

Stiffly Webb swung to the ground. Saddles creaked as other riders did the same. Webb looped his reins over a rail, swallowed, then stepped through the front door out of the heat, into the deep shadow behind the thick adobe walls.

Florentino limped out from behind the counter. "Mister Webb, you catch Donovan, maybe?"

Webb shook his head and dropped his chin. "Almost, Florentino. He got to the river ahead of us."

Florentino said solemnly, "Too bad." He paused. "How about Aparicio? He's one good tracker, *si?* Did he do you a good job?"

Webb looked at the hard-packed dirt floor. "He did us a fine job."

With pride the Mexican said, "I told you. He's one good boy, that Aparicio." He looked over the men's silent faces. "Where is he? Did he not come home?"

Webb's hands flexed nervously. "He came home. He's outside." Florentino moved toward the door. Webb caught the Mexican's shoulder, stopping him. "Florentino!" He looked the man in the eyes, and he saw sudden alarm in Florentino's face. Webb said sorrowfully, "I hate to tell you. He's dead."

The Mexican stood in shock, his dark face unbelieving. Stiffly then he limped out the door into the sunshine. He stared dry-eyed at the body tied across the horse.

"Who is kill him? Donovan?"

"A Mexican officer did the shootin'. Donovan was the cause of it." Quietly he recounted the events that led up to Aparicio's death. Florentino listened with a deep sadness in his eyes.

"A good boy, Aparicio," he said finally. "But very young, and maybeso a little foolish. Please, you will help me take him into the house?"

Carefully they untied Aparicio and carried him into the living quarters behind the store. Webb heard a cry and saw Florentino's wife, Consuela, sit up in bed, staring in horror. Florentino said to her, *"Es Aparicio."* She began to sob. For the first time Webb saw the tiny bundle lying beside her. Her movement awakened the newly-born child, and it began to whimper.

Webb said, "I see the baby got here."

Florentino nodded grimly. "One is born, another dies."

"Named it yet?"

Florentino shook his head. "We could not decide. Now, I think, there is no question." He looked bleakly at the baby. "We will call him Aparicio."

From there they rode on to Quince's livery stable and un-saddled. Juan Obregon, a gray-haired Mexican who had been watching the place for Quince, took care of the horses as the men released them. He put out some grain for them—not too much, for this was summertime, and grain made for heat.

Webb said to Quince, "Juan's some kin to Aparicio and Florentino, isn't he?"

"An uncle, I think. I better break the news to him."

Webb nodded. "Boy died in the line of duty. Tell Juan I reckon the county will pay his buryin'. If it don't, *I* will. He deserves more than just bein' wrapped in an old blanket and covered over with dirt."

Quince said, "We'll *all* help pay for it." He paused, his face clouding. "And Donovan will pay for it too, one of these days."

From the livery barn it wasn't far up to the hill where the town's cemetery was. Drawn there, Webb stood awhile among the crosses and leaning headstones, staring at the small mound where they had buried someone and called him Donovan, so many years ago. He looked at the wooden cross with the words CLABE DONOVAN printed across it in peeling black paint.

"Clabe," Webb said quietly, absently, "if it's not you down there, then who in hell is it?"

He wanted desperately to see Ellie Donovan, but to do so now would only cause pain, and for no good reason. He gathered clean clothes from his office, noting that nothing had been touched while he had been gone. Sandy hadn't been back. Well, Webb hadn't really expected him, not this soon. Maybe not at all.

He walked down to the barber shop to clean up. Afterwards he carried his dirty clothes across to the widow Sanchez, as was his custom. He could tell by the old woman's manner that she already knew about Aparicio. By now the word had had time to spread all over the Mexican settlement. There would be much grief down there, for the boy hadn't had an enemy.

Looked like, sometimes, the good ones died young while the Donovans of the world lived on forever.

Walking back, Webb took a long look at Ellie's Dry Fork cafe, wishing . . .

He shook his head. Idle to think about it. No need in a man punishing himself like that.

To his surprise he found Ellie pacing the floor in his office, waiting for him. After staring a moment, speechless, he finally said, "Never expected to see you here, Ellie. Figured you'd be at the cafe, gettin' supper ready."

"It can wait," she said thinly. From the dark hollows beneath her eyes, he could tell she hadn't slept much lately. A brooding anxiety showed in her face. He took a step forward as if to take her in his arms, then stopped. She said, "I heard a little of the rumor that worked down the street a while ago. You didn't catch Clabe."

He shook his head. "No."

She dropped her chin. "I don't know whether I'm glad or not. I wish I *did* know." She paused. "I'm sorry about that Mexican boy. Folks say he was a nice boy."

He nodded, studying her face, an ache twisting inside him like a knife blade. He said, "That makes another thing Clabe Donovan will have to pay for. Sooner or later we *will* catch him, Ellie. You've got to prepare yourself for that."

She didn't reply. She was in misery, yet she didn't cry. Probably she had cried herself out.

He went on, "Long as he stays out loose, more people are goin' to die. First was old Joe Vickers—as good a man as ever drew a breath. And then that Rodriguez boy, shot for no reason. No, not by Clabe himself, but on account of Clabe. It won't end there. The only way to stop it is to stop Clabe." He hesitated, wishing he could avoid what he was about to say. "Ellie, even if you do still love him, you're bound to see that he's got to be brought in, else there'll be others. You could help."

She raised her eyes to him. "How?"

"Clabe used the same hideout down there all the time you lived with him, didn't he?"

She nodded.

He said, "It stands to reason he's likely usin' it again. Now, we can't go into Mexico and search him out. The Mexican cavalry wouldn't allow us that much time. But if we knew right where to go, we might cross at night, grab him and bring him back across the river before that trigger-happy Armendariz knew what had happened. You could tell us, Ellie."

Ellie Donovan had been standing up all this time. Now, suddenly, she sank into a chair. "Webb, do you know what you're asking of me?"

He nodded soberly. "I do, Ellie. I'm not sayin' you have to, not even sayin' I *want* you to. But it's a way to put an end to all this. You'll have to make up your own mind. I don't aim to pressure you."

For a long time she sat there, her face in her hands. When finally she looked up, she was still dry-eyed. She shook her head. "Whatever he's done, however bad he's become, he's still my husband. I'd do anything else—even go down there myself and plead with him. But this . . ." Again she shook her head. "I couldn't do it, Webb. Please don't ask me."

He studied her gravely. "All right, Ellie. Forget I said anything."

She stood up to go. Again he felt a desperate yearning to take her into his arms. He put his hands behind him and turned half around, away from her. "I wish there was somethin' I could do, Ellie, somethin' I could say."

She replied quietly, "There isn't, Webb. I suppose this is as hard for you, in a way, as it is for me. You coming over for supper later?"

"No, I thought it'd be better if I took my meals over at the Dutchman's awhile. Be better for both of us, Ellie."

"It would, Webb. Goodbye."

She stepped out into the street and was gone.

She hadn't been out of the place more than a couple of minutes when Judge Upshaw arrived, nervous as a condemned man. One look and Webb knew he was in for a wrangle.

"You let him get through your fingers, didn't you?" Upshaw exclaimed.

Seated at his desk, Webb didn't stand up or offer the judge a chair. "If you've heard that much, you've heard enough to know the cards were stacked against us. We couldn't stay across the river."

"Maybe you didn't really want to catch him."

Webb's teeth clamped together. "You're workin' up to somethin', judge. Say it plain."

"All right, I will. Maybe you're afraid of him. Or maybe it's something else. A long time ago, you were friends with Clabe Donovan. Even now you share a common interest . . . perhaps a more common interest than we've supposed."

Webb stiffened. "Watch out, judge."

"I saw her leave here just now. Didn't waste much time getting together with her after you came in, did you? Did she promise you anything if you wouldn't catch up with her husband?"

Webb pushed to his feet and took a step toward the judge, his fist clenched. "Call me anything you want to, judge; you've already done it often enough. But say another word about Ellie Donovan and I'll drag you through that street on your face!"

The judge shrank back and swallowed, but he had a deeper fear of Clabe Donovan than of Webb Matlock. "Dammit, man," the jurist said, "you know what Donovan swore to do. You ought to know better than anybody why he's got to be brought in."

Webb loosened a little. He realized that the tight grip of fear was on the judge, making him say things he probably wouldn't otherwise. Even the bravest man might lose sleep over the thought of an outlaw coming back from the grave to carry out a promise of vengeance, made years ago. And Judge Upshaw was not a brave man. A shuddering dread had eroded his reason.

"We'll bring him in, judge," Webb promised. "Somehow, we'll get him!"

7

FOR A TIME THEN, NOTHING WAS HEARD OF DONOVAN. SO
far as anyone at Dry Fork knew, he made no effort to
cross the river. With a grimly single-minded purpose, Johnny
Willet had begun a one-man patrol on a long section of the
river. He put in a hard ride from his starting point at daylight
each morning, stopping at noon where he had kept a few
extra horses in a little valley that had some decent grass. He
would eat a cold meal, carried with him all morning, put his
saddle on a fresh horse and start back, covering the same
ground twice a day, diligently watching for tracks. At night
he slept in a tiny abandoned rock house built long ago by a
venturesome Mexican family which finally withdrew because
of Indians and never came back. The house had only half a
roof, but at this time of year it didn't rain much anyway.

One day the mail brought cryptic letters to several people
in town. Webb got one of them. His was simply a piece of
paper with a skull and crossbones penciled on it, and the
word SOON scrawled beneath the picture. Quince Pyburn
received a similar one. Judge Upshaw staggered to Webb's
office and with trembling hands gave Webb the one he had
received. It bore a picture of a hangman's knot and noose.
The judge's face had turned almost as white as the paper.

"It's from Donovan," he croaked. "He's going to kill me,

Matlock. He's going to kill me unless you give me protection. I *demand* protection."

"Several people got letters like that today," Webb told him. "Every one of them deserves protection. But the only way I could guarantee it is to put all of you in a jail cell together where I could keep watch on the whole bunch at one time."

"It's your duty to protect me. I'm an officer of the court."

"It's my job to protect everybody, but there's a point where I can do just so much and no more. Everybody's got to help take care of himself."

Tears showed in the judge's eyes. "You're going to let him kill me, Matlock. You're just going to stand there and let him come to kill me!"

He weaved out the front door, braced himself a moment on a post, then made his way down the street toward his house.

The judge had left his letter behind. Webb studied it, face twisting as he looked for something he could put his finger on. Far as he could tell, it had been drawn by the same hand which had prepared the others Webb had seen. Postmark was the same on all of them—Rio Escondido. That was a railroad town forty miles northeast, much farther from the Rio Grande than Dry Fork was. Unlikely that Donovan had been up there himself. Probably he had had someone do the task for him.

Webb became certain of it when Bronc Tomlin came through town, headed toward his ranch with a fresh suit of clothes, a shave, haircut and a red-haired saloon girl folks said he had just brought from Rio Escondido. That was a larger and busier town than Dry Fork. It was where Bronc usually went periodically when he wanted feminine company to share his ranchhouse a while. It afforded more selection. Besides, the few Dry Fork girls who would even consider the type of proposition Bronc made knew Bronc's place by now. They wouldn't go for love or money.

Webb was almost certain Bronc had mailed the letters. After checking with Ellie and learning that the writing was not Clabe Donovan's, Webb decided Bronc had even done the drawings himself. He had no doubt that the work had been done at Donovan's request, though.

"You ain't goin' to arrest him?" Quince Pyburn asked incredulously as the two of them watched Bronc's buckboard roll dustily down the trail toward the Rafter T.

Webb shook his head. "What could I prove on him? When I put Bronc Tomlin in that jailhouse, I want to know I can keep him."

One afternoon Johnny Willet rode into town on a sweat-lathered horse so exhausted it stood and trembled at the hitchrack while Johnny sprinted onto the porch and into Webb's office. Webb looked up in surprise. Seeing the excitement in Johnny's eyes, he wasted no time in foolish questions.

"Donovan?"

Johnny nodded and braced himself against Webb's desk. He was too worn out to stand steady. "I think so, Webb." He weaved across the room to a water pitcher. Thirstily he emptied the dipper twice, then poured another dipperful over his head, letting the water run off into a tin washbasin. He sank into a chair, breathing a long, weary sigh.

"I think he's fixin' to come across the river. May already be over, headin' for Rio Escondido. Yesterday three men swam the *rio*, two white men and a Mexican. All of a sudden I got the idea they were Donovan men. I took and followed them all the way to Bronc Tomlin's. I laid up on a rise and watched them through my spyglass. They gathered a bunch of horses. Then, with a couple of Bronc's men to help them, they commenced pushin' the horses to the northeast. I followed, a good ways back. About twenty miles from Tomlin's, they dropped off six head. One of the Tomlin men stayed to loose-herd them on grass around a hole of water. Another twenty miles or so, they done the same thing again. When I left to come here, they had six horses left and was pushin' them on in the direction of Rio Escondido.

"It come to me, Webb, that they was settin' up a relay of fresh horses. Does that mean to you what it meant to me?"

Excitement began to rise in Webb. "A raid on Rio Escondido! Bank, most likely. When they're through they can head south and have fresh horses all the way back to the Rio Grande."

Johnny nodded. "That's what it looked like to me."

Standing up, Webb glanced toward his gun cabinet. "I sure wish we had a telegraph line from here to Rio Escondido." He unsnapped the padlock that held a bar in front of the guns. "Only way to get a message there is to take it. Think you're up to another ride?"

"For a chance at Donovan? I'd go bareback, plumb to the Mississippi River."

The rifles were loaded. Webb kept them that way, even though they weren't used much anymore. "Take your horse over to Quince's, Johnny. Tell him what's up. Tell him I'm goin' to gather some men and be over there in a few minutes. May need to use some of his horses."

Tired though he was, Johnny Willet stepped out of the office in long strides. He mounted and urged the weary horse up the street.

Webb sat at his desk just long enough to pen a short note. He knew it might take hours to round up a large posse such as he ought to have. He must settle for what he could get. He walked up the street, looking in every place he came to for men he had confidence in, men he felt were stable enough for the job. He avoided any he feared might be trigger-happy. They were even worse than the gun-shy kind. By the time Webb reached Quince's, he had picked nearly a dozen men. Some who had horses handy went to fetch them. Others hurried to Quince's afoot to see what the stableman could offer.

Among the people gathered at the livery barn was Quince's sixteen-year-old nephew. Webb didn't want any kids along on a mission like this. "Billy," he said, "I got a mighty important job for you." He took out the note he had written. "Ride to Rio Escondido as fast as you can. Don't kill your horse, but don't hold back any more than you have to. Find the sheriff and tell him we think Clabe Donovan is fixin' to pay him a call. Give him this note. He knows my handwritin', and he'll know you're tellin' him the truth. Tell him we know where the relay horses are posted, and we're goin' to try to stop Donovan before he ever gets to Rio Escondido. A gunfight in town is too risky to women and kids. But tell him he better be ready in case we miss."

A little disappointed, the boy nodded. "If you want me to, Webb. Only, I was sure hopin' . . ."

"This is a serious responsibility I'm handin' you, Billy. You're light and can make a fast ride. I wouldn't give the job to just anybody."

The compliment paid off. Beaming, Billy swung onto his horse and left town in a lope. He sat straight and proud in the saddle.

Johnny Willet came back from the general store with a pack of supplies tied across the back of a led horse. "Ready whenever you are, Webb," he said. The deputy was tired, but he wouldn't back down.

Webb said, "Let's go."

It hadn't been half an hour since Johnny had arrived in town. Now he and Webb were heading out again with Quince Pyburn and nearly a dozen men following in an easy lope. Off to meet Clabe Donovan . . .

The second group of Donovan relay horses had been placed at a fairly well-known landmark, several grand old cottonwood trees marking a spring that had not been known to go dry in even the droughtiest years. It was a logical place because Donovan, possessing an old familiarity with the country, would not have trouble finding it, even hard pressed by pursuit.

A mile from the spring, Webb held up his hand and told the possemen to dismount so they would not easily be seen. To Johnny he said, "Let's me and you go scout the situation."

Circling the spring, they came up from the hilly side where they wouldn't be spotted. The tops of the cottonwoods showed above the hills where the two men tied their horses to set out afoot. Webb removed his spurs and hung them on the saddlehorn so they wouldn't jingle while he walked, or trip him as he climbed the hill. Johnny followed suit. Webb slipped his saddlegun out of its scabbard and started to climb. Again Johnny followed his example. The cowboy was a fair shot with a rifle, but with a pistol he couldn't hit a barn from the inside with all the doors shut.

The top of the hill was almost bare of vegetation. Grass and weeds had burned to a brittle brown in the sun. Webb took off his hat which might show conspicuously against the skyline. He dropped to his hands and knees, easing in behind a small clump of hardy *guajilla*. Johnny inched up beside him. In both men had lurked an unspoken fear that they might have arrived too late, that Donovan might already have passed this way.

Johnny had brought his spyglass with him, but there was no need for it. They could see readily enough that six hobbled horses grazed near the spring. One man waited down there in the shade of the cottonwoods, a rifle across his lap and his hat down over his eyes. He appeared to be dozing in the summer heat.

"We could slip down there and take him," Johnny suggested.

Webb shook his head. "We'll leave things alone. When Donovan rides in, we want to have everything lookin' natural. We'll catch them while they're unsaddlin', maybe set some of them afoot."

Johnny said, "From here, if the breaks come right, it'll be like shootin' fish in a barrel."

Webb saw an eagerness in the cowboy's eyes. He remembered how Johnny had sickened after having to kill his first man—that young rustler who had been wounded while running off some of Jess Leggett's cows. Johnny had hated the thought of killing, then. Now he had had reason enough to change. He had seen two men die because of Donovan—Uncle Joe Vickers and Aparicio.

Webb thought fleetingly of Ellie Donovan, and he wished things could have turned out some other way. "I hope when the time comes, Johnny, it isn't me who has to kill Clabe."

From the hilltop he had a fair command of the surrounding countryside. He could see fairly clearly to the south across the scattering of mesquite, the stunty green *guajilla*, all the way to where the horizon line shimmered in the sun. He whispered, "You stay here and keep your eyes peeled, Johnny. I'll go back and fetch the rest of the boys in closer."

Using the roundabout approach, out of sight of the lone man who took care of the horses, Webb brought his posse in behind the hill. From his position he could make out Johnny, still bellied down. Johnny shook his head as if to say he had seen nothing yet. Webb nodded and turned to the possemen. "We'd just as well settle down for a wait. No tellin' when Donovan is liable to show up."

He expected the outlaw to appear before long. It didn't stand to reason Donovan would send these horses very far ahead of him; too much chance of somebody coming across them and getting suspicious. But the minutes stretched into hours, and Webb saw no sign. He and Johnny Willet remained on top of the hill, watching. At intervals Webb took Johnny's spyglass and carefully swept the horizon, looking for sign of dust or of moving figures. Nothing.

Night came. The man at the spring built a small fire and began to boil coffee in a can. The pleasant smell of it drifted up and set Webb's stomach to stirring. He said, "Johnny, ease down and tell the boys they can fix some coffee if they want it. Just a small fire, though. That feller couldn't smell it over his own."

Johnny said with gratitude, "Sure suits me. I got a terrible cravin'." He hesitated about moving down off the hill. "Webb, I figured they'd get here before now. Reckon somethin' went wrong?"

Webb could see worry in Johnny's eyes. The same worry had begun to gnaw at Webb, too. "All we can do is wait. He might've figured on hittin' Rio Escondido at night, maybe to blow the safe. You never can tell what a man like Clabe Donovan is liable to do. You just have to wait and be ready."

Johnny left. Before long Webb could see the dim flicker of a small fire where the possemen waited. They had dug a hole and built the fire in it. From ground level, it wouldn't be visible very far. After a long time Johnny came back, and

Webb was able to go back down the hill. The men at the bottom sat around silently sipping hot coffee. Webb could hardly see them in the darkness. Quince Pyburn had kicked sand over the small fire once it was no longer needed. Now there was not even a glow. Quince handed Webb a cup. He said nothing, but Webb could sense in the tall man the same plaguing doubt that he felt in himself.

"Quince, you're thinkin' we might've made a wrong guess."

Quince shook his head. "I don't know how we could have. A blind man could see what Donovan sent these horses for. But . . ."

"But what?"

"Maybe somethin' changed Clabe's plans. Maybe somethin' boogered him." Quince finished his coffee. He let the dregs and the last drops drip out into the dirt.

Webb said, "You never can be sure of anything, Quince. You just use your judgment and take your choice and hope it works out. No man can do more than that." He stood up. "I'm goin' back up that hill. You fellers try to get you some sleep. Could be a long night."

It *was* a long night, a terribly long night. Webb stayed atop the hill with Johnny, dozing occasionally when he knew Johnny was awake. But even dozing, he was never far from consciousness. He heard every stamp of a horse's foot, heard the thin snore of the lone man who waited at the spring. When the first flush of dawn spread in the east, he opened his burning eyes and squinted across the rolling land to the south.

He saw nothing.

Below, the man with the horses awakened and rebuilt his burned-out fire. In a little while he had coffee going and was frying bacon in a small skillet. The smell of it stirred hunger in Webb. It also awakened a strong doubt.

Donovan should have been here before this.

On the other side of the hill, the possemen moved with caution, making no noise. Webb sent Johnny down to eat. Later, when Johnny returned, Webb went down.

Webb had only half finished his coffee when Johnny signaled him excitedly. Webb dropped his cup in the grass and hurried up the hill. Lying flat on his stomach, Johnny pointed. Webb saw a single rider moving toward the spring, coming from the southwest. He took out the spyglass and focused on the man. He thought this was another Tomlin rider.

The horseman drew up at the spring and swung down with a wave of his hand. The man who had kept the horses was standing, waiting. He motioned the newcomer to the fire and poured coffee for him. Webb could hear the low murmur of their conversation, but he couldn't make out a word of it.

The rider ate a little. He caught a fresh horse, leaving his own, then waved to the other man and started out again, heading northeast.

"Goin' toward the place where they left the next bunch of horses," Johnny observed.

"I'd give a lot to know what kind of message he brought with him."

"We could catch him and find out."

"No, best we let them play out the string their own way."

The man by the spring began leisurely gathering up what little camp gear he had. He rolled his blanket and tied it behind his saddle. He caught one of the horses, saddled him, then began removing the hobbles from the others. Moving slowly, as if he had the rest of the year to do it in, he swung up and began pushing the horses southwestward.

Incredulous, Johnny exclaimed, "Webb, he's takin' them horses home!"

Webb swore. "There's a skunk in the woods someplace. Come on, we'll find out what it is."

Moving down the hillside, he signaled the possemen to their horses. By the time he and Johnny got there, the men were tightening their cinches and getting ready to ride. Excitedly Quince Pyburn asked, "Donovan?"

Webb shook his head. "Feller's leavin' with the horses. Somethin's gone wrong, and I want to know what."

He led out in a hard lope that soon had the men spurring to catch up with him. Johnny Willet rode half a length behind, the other possemen followed in a ragged pattern. The man with the loose horses had a quarter-mile head start, but it didn't last long. A mile from the spring, Webb Matlock overtook him. The rider looked back and drew rein. He faced around and waited, letting his horses work on ahead. They moved along in a steady trot as if they enjoyed being free of the hobbles and moving toward the home range they knew. Horses, like many people, had a powerful homing instinct.

Webb stopped. The rider who faced him was in his early twenties, shaggy-haired and needing a shave. Webb had seen him in town with Bronc Tomlin. Clinch, his name was. An insolent amusement played in the cowboy's pale eyes. He glanced at the pistol on Webb's hip and at the saddlegun.

"You're sure packin' the hardware, sheriff. Goin' to a shootin' match someplace?"

"Where you takin' those horses?" Webb demanded.

"Home, sheriff, that's all. Back to Bronc Tomlin's. Bronc's broncs, these are."

The other possemen began to catch up. They formed a half circle around the Tomlin man, their faces grim. Webb caught a momentary flicker of fear in the young rider's eyes, a lapse quickly corrected. The cowboy managed somehow to grin. It was plainly forced, but a grin nevertheless.

Webb asked harshly, "What were you doin' out here?"

"Any law against a man travelin', sheriff?"

"Depends on where he's goin' and what he figures on doin' when he gets there. How come you to hold those horses at the spring?"

"Because that's where the water was. Some grass too." Clinch seemed to enjoy his innocent answers. "Wouldn't want me to camp where the horses couldn't get no feed or water, would you?"

"You know that's not what I meant. What were you here for in the first place? Doesn't make sense, bringin' horses all the way here from the Rafter T and then takin' them right back again."

"Ain't no law says a man has got to make sense all the time, sheriff."

Angered, Webb said, "*You'd* better start makin' sense!"

For a minute Clinch sat there, his grin fading, his eyes turning hostile. Then, silently, Quince Pyburn loosened his hornstring and took his rope loose from the horn. Coolly he built a small loop in it and looked toward Clinch. He spoke not a word, but his eyes carried a strong message.

The rider swallowed. He began to break. "Now look, sheriff, you know I ain't done nothin'. All I done was to bring them horses out here, just like Bronc Tomlin told me to. Said a buyer might show up, wantin' them. Nobody did, and while ago one of the boys came and told me Bronc said bring the horses home." He looked around nervously. "Ain't nothin' wrong in that. I'm workin' for wages and I do what I'm told to. Any complaint you got, you go take it up with Bronc Tomlin."

Webb sat rigid in the saddle, leaning forward on stiffened arms, his hands on the horn. He glared in helpless anger. Finally he jerked his head abruptly. "Go on, then. Get out of here!"

Quince Pyburn protested, "Webb, you lettin' him go?"

"Have to. We can't show that there's been a law broken."

"We know they figured on it."

"It's not what we know to our own satisfaction that counts; it's what we can convince a jury of."

"It's a hell of a note, that's all I can say."

"Quince, the law's written so that the guilty ones slip through sometimes. But it's got to be that way to protect the innocent. If we go stretchin' it to get at those we know are guilty, it can someday backfire against those who are innocent. Better to let a dozen badmen get away than to hang one man who didn't deserve it."

He reined his horse around and headed him toward Dry Fork.

A vague prescience came to him like a cold hand across his throat long before the posse got back to town. For no solid reason, a terrible feeling grew in him that something had gone badly wrong. When he reined off the trail and into the dusty street, he knew. He could see it in the silent faces that stared at him and his posse.

The word of their arrival preceded them up the street. Ellie

Donovan stepped out onto the porch of her restaurant. As the riders neared, she walked into the street and stood waiting for Webb.

Webb swung stiffly out of the saddle. He looked down into her anxious eyes. "What is it, Ellie? What's happened?"

"Trouble, Webb. Some of it's already over with, and some is waiting for you. The bank was robbed late yesterday afternoon."

Stunned, Webb let his lips move in an oath that didn't come out loud. He glanced down at her again, hating what he had to ask her.

"Clabe?"

"They said it was."

Webb clenched his fists futilely. How could he have figured wrong? It didn't make sense.

"Anybody hurt?" he asked.

She shook her head. "They fired bullets into Judge Upshaw's house but didn't hit him. He came out later with lint all over him. He'd been under the bed."

"You didn't see Clabe yourself? He didn't even ride by your place?"

She said, "No."

Clabe had changed a lot, Webb thought. Strange the man would ride into the town where his wife lived—a wife like Ellie—and not even try to see her. *In his place*, he told himself, *I'd even have taken her with me, whether she wanted to go or not.*

He said, "Thanks, Ellie. I better get on down to the bank."

She looked as if she had something else to say but was afraid to bring it out. Finally: "Webb, there's something else . . . something I can't tell you. Don't you believe it. Don't let yourself believe it."

She turned quickly away. He called, "Ellie . . ." She didn't stop. She entered the small restaurant without looking back at him.

Now that cold feeling lay like a chunk of lead in the pit of his stomach. A little sick with dread, he swung back into the saddle and moved on toward the bank. In front of it, waiting for him, stood Judge Upshaw, banker William Freeman, and half a dozen others, all prominent in business or politics. All were gravely silent except the judge. Upshaw said caustically, "Well, sheriff, you finally got here. Almost a day late."

Webb wished he had a good answer, but he didn't; so he kept his mouth shut and tried to hold down the resentment that flared in him against the judge.

Banker Freeman gazed at Webb with no evident ill will. Almost, there was sorrow in his eyes. "Some of us got up a posse of sorts, Webb, but we didn't do much good. The best men in town were with you."

Webb said regretfully, "I did what looked like the best thing at the time. How bad was the damage?"

"Not as bad as it could've been. They hit late in the afternoon. They rode into town firing their guns to scare people off of the streets and out of the way, the way they say Jesse James used to do it. I knew what was coming. I had half a minute to grab up most of the money and shove it away in some desk drawers. I told them they had come too late—that I'd just sent a shipment of money to the big bank in Rio Escondido. They believed me. They took what they could find and left with it. Twenty-five hundred—maybe $3000."

Webb asked, "It *was* Clabe Donovan?"

Freeman nodded. "They wore masks, Webb, all of them. But the leader of the bunch had all the old Donovan trademarks—the build, the voice, the black sombrero. It was a little eerie, like seeing a ghost."

"An awfully live ghost," Webb gritted. "They got across the Rio Grande, I expect."

Freeman said, "They were headed in that direction. We trailed them a while, but they fired on us, and we knew we weren't the kind of posse that could stop them. No use getting somebody killed. We gave up and came back."

"You did the right thing," Webb said. "I wish I had been here."

Freeman frowned darkly. "Webb, in a way you'd best be glad you weren't."

"What do you mean?"

Freeman had trouble framing the words for a reply.

Judge Upshaw said, "Where's that brother of yours, sheriff?"

"I don't know."

Upshaw snorted, "You don't know, but *we* know."

Flame came in Webb's cheeks. "Stop talkin' in circles, judge. What's this about Sandy?"

The banker cut Upshaw off with a sharp look. "Let me handle it, judge. You've got about as much tact as a black Mexican bull." He turned back to Webb, his face heavy with regret. "Four of them came into the bank—Donovan and three more. One stayed at the front door, and the last one held the horses. They had just gotten the money and were fixing to go when the mask slipped on one outlaw's face. I got a good look. So did Jake Scully, who happened to be in here at the time. It was Augie Brock, the kid who always pals around with your brother Sandy."

Webb felt the rest coming. "Sandy and Augie haven't been together in a good while."

"Can you say for sure, Webb? You haven't seen Sandy lately." Freeman's chin dropped and he added slowly, "One of the other outlaws stayed right by Augie during the holdup. He wore a mask and didn't say a word, but I could tell he was young, about the same age as Augie. About the same age as Sandy too, Webb. Same age, same height, same build. Jake and I compared notes after the ruckus. Neither one of us could get on a witness stand and swear to it, but we agreed that other boy could have been Sandy!"

Webb swayed.

The banker said, "I'm sorry, Webb. I can only tell you what I saw."

"But you didn't see Sandy. You couldn't have!"

Freeman said evenly, "He's always been a wild sort of a boy. Even you will admit that."

"Wild, sure, but not an outlaw. You know he's not an outlaw!"

Freeman looked down. "I'd be pleased to find out I was wrong, Webb. I'm sorry."

He turned with slumped shoulders and walked back into the bank.

Webb took a deep breath, but there was nothing to say.

Judge Upshaw said, "One more thing you ought to know, sheriff. I've sent for the Rangers. We've got to bring this thing to an end."

He turned and walked away, leaving Webb to stand alone.

8

WEBB SAW LITTLE TO BE GAINED IN TAKING A POSSE OUT on Donovan's trail, or even in following it himself. Donovan had surely gone across the river hours ago. Moreover, Webb's possemen were already tired from their fruitless mission.

Webb was still puzzled over that mission. It seemed unlikely the outlaw had gone to all that trouble just in hope he could lead the sheriff astray. If Johnny Willet hadn't elected to follow the Bronc Tomlin horses, Webb wouldn't have been out of Dry Fork when the raiders hit the bank. Any number of things could have gone wrong if this had been an actual plan of Donovan's. Webb felt sure the man had really intended to use those horses in a ride to Rio Escondido. Somehow at the last minute he had switched his plans.

Why? That question kept nagging Webb as he slumped exhausted in his chair at the office and stared absently at a crack in the wall.

Preying on his mind even more was the question of Sandy. That was something else that didn't make sense. Granted that Sandy had always been hard to handle, more prone than most to take the bit in his teeth and run with it. Granted that it was in his nature to be a rebel. He still wasn't an outlaw, not a thief, not a robber of banks. Webb conceded that he hadn't understood his brother. Still, he thought he knew him this well. He thought he had pounded at least that much of his own and his parents' ideas of right and wrong into the boy's head.

Webb hadn't realized how weary he was, having ridden so far, having only dozed occasionally through last night. Sitting still, he dropped off to sleep in the chair. He didn't awaken until he felt someone's hand lightly touch his shoulder. Startled, he jerked himself erect, blinking. He was surprised to find that night had come. The office was dark. Outside, lamps glowed in the buildings up and down the street.

"Didn't mean to drop off to sleep," Webb said, still a little loggy. "Can't see you in the dark. Who is it?"

"It's me, Quince." Quince Pyburn struck a match and held it. Webb reached to his desk and removed the glass chimney from a lamp. He held the lamp out for Quince to light. He trimmed the burning wick to suit him and set the chimney back in place. Then he rubbed his eyes.

"I feel like a fool, Quince, goin' off to sleep like this when I ought to be out doin' somethin' about Donovan. Only, what could I do?"

Quince pulled up a rawhide chair. "Nothin'. You'd just as well catch up on your rest. At least *that* will do you some good."

Webb stared somberly at the dancing shadows cast on the wall by the flickering lamp. "You've heard what they said about Sandy?"

Quince frowned, taking a long time before he came up with an answer. When he did, it was straight and honest. "I've heard. I'm not sayin' it was him. I *am* sayin' it *could be*. He's always been a little on the salty side, Webb. He may have looked like you, but he never did think the same way."

"He wasn't *that* different, Quince."

"Remember, he left here mad, wantin' to show you he was his own man. Boy with that kind of attitude is liable to make a mistake just out of orneriness."

Webb blinked his burning eyes and kept his gaze away from Quince. Quince paused a long time, then added, "Keep on hopin' it wasn't him, Webb. But be ready to take it in case it was." He placed his hand on Webb's shoulder. That's more or less the reason I came over here. Thought you ought to know the talk that's been goin' on up the street."

"Talk?"

"Well, a little. Most of it's comin' from one man, and I don't have to tell you his name. His initials are Judge Upshaw."

Webb swore. "That fathead! What's he been sayin'?"

Quince shrugged. "Without me havin' to tell you, I think you can pretty well guess what he's been sayin' about Sandy. Johnny Willet and me, we went into Jake Scully's place while ago for a drink. Kind of felt like we needed one. The judge was there talkin'—he's always talkin', seems like. Talkin' about Sandy some, sayin' things had come to a pretty pass when the sheriff's own brother would go to the bad like that. Said a man who would let a brother grow up and take to the back trails didn't deserve no badge.

"Well, mostly it was like that for a while. Didn't seem like the boys was payin' him much mind anyway, so we just sat and kept our mouths shut. Then he commenced to talk about Ellie Donovan."

Webb straightened in anger. "That foul-mouthed . . ."

Quince held up his hand. "Now, just wait a minute before you jump out there and make a racket. Let me tell you the rest of it." Webb sat down, his face burning. Quince said, "He pointed out that Ellie is Clabe Donovan's wife. Said all these years we thought she was a widow, he would bet she knew different. He would bet she'd been sittin' here spyin' on us, waitin' to tell him when the time was right for him to come back. Even stringin' the sheriff along, pullin' the wool over his eyes, which wasn't hard to do. Man like Webb Matlock could be easy swayed by a fetchin' woman, the judge said."

Webb stood up so fast that the chair fell back against the wall. He reached for his hat. Quince Pyburn caught Webb's arm. "Now, hold on. Johnny and me, we took care of the judge. When he said what he did about Ellie, we decided he'd gone as far as any right-thinkin' man could allow. You remember them wooden pegs Jake Scully has driven into his walls for people to hang their hats and coats on? Well, me and Johnny, we picked the judge up and hung him on a peg by his collar. We told Jake Scully if he lifted the judge down we would put *him* there in his place. Jake just grinned and said he never bothered anything his customers hung up."

Webb said grimly, "I wish *I* had been there . . ."

"Better that you weren't. A man belittles himself to get mixed up in a barroom argument thataway. You might've caused a lot of smoke and made some folks begin to think maybe the judge had a point. Way it was, everybody got a big laugh out of it—everybody but the judge."

Webb stood and fumed and flexed his hands. But finally the first flush of anger passed, and he could see Quince was talking sense to him. "I thank you, Quince. You did right. But I reckon I still better do some talkin' to the judge."

Quince looked at him questioningly, and Webb shook his head. "No smoke, Quince. Just a little talk."

"Promise?"

"I promise."

He was still weary, and his steps were short as he worked his way down the lamp-lighted street, pausing to glance inside each saloon. When he came to Jake Scully's, he stopped and peered over the swinging doors, looking first at the row of pegs. Somebody had taken the judge down from the wall. Jake, wiping the bar, spotted Webb standing outside. Sensing Webb's mission, he slowly shook his head and pointed on down the street. Webb gave him a short wave of his hand and went on.

Jake's was the last bar. The judge must have gone home. Webb walked across to Upshaw's house. At first he thought the place was dark. Then he could make out a faint glow of light at the bottom of the door. Webb remembered someone telling him that the judge had nailed blankets over the windows after the first Donovan scare.

Must have been insufferably hot in that house with the windows covered and the doors closed, Webb reflected. Summer wasn't this country's most comfortable season even with the windows open. But the judge was more interested in preservation than in comfort.

Webb knocked briskly on the front door. He heard a sudden noise, a chair sliding back across the floor. He had probably frightened the judge half out of his wits. "Judge," Webb called, "open up."

He hadn't tested the doorknob, but he was sure without doing so that the door was firmly locked. It was probably also barred from the inside.

A quavering voice asked, "Who is it? Who's out yonder?"

"Webb Matlock."

There was a moment of silence. Then: "What do you want with me, sheriff?"

"Just want to talk a little, is all."

"Go away. Go away."

"I'm not goin' to hurt you, judge. I just think it's time we did a little talkin', you and me. I'm goin' to do it even if I have to break that door down."

Another moment of indecisive quiet, then footsteps sounded on the floor. Webb heard the clink of a key in the lock and the sliding of a bar from its place. "Come on in, then," Upshaw said.

Webb pushed the door open. The judge stood back out of reach, leaning with his left hand on a table while his shaking right hand gripped a pistol. It was pointed vaguely in Webb's direction. "Step inside and shut the door," the judge said. "Don't want anybody to be able to get a shot at me in here. Then you just stop where you are. Don't you come one step closer to me."

Webb glanced around him, almost sickening at the hot, foul air, the closeness of a room shut up for days in the stifling heat of summer. He caught the strong smell of whisky. Webb could see a bottle and a half-empty glass on the table, near Upshaw's hand. He knew then where the judge got what little courage it took for him to stand and hold the pistol.

Webb said, "You can put that cannon away. I don't aim to dirty my hands."

Warily the judge lowered the pistol. He held onto it a

moment before he finally laid it on the table. He picked up the glass and swallowed in one gulp the whisky that remained in it. Then he sank into his chair. The man was trembling. In the flickering lamplight Webb could see the dark hollows beneath the judge's eyes, the sallow color of his cheeks. Upshaw hadn't slept much lately. Mostly he had kept himself locked in this fetid room, eating too little, drinking too much, letting his mind run riot with all manner of dark fears.

Webb stared, and slowly most of the things he had intended to say lost their importance. He could almost feel sorry for this wretched little man who slacked here in fearful misery.

"Judge, I came to scorch your hide for the things you've said about Sandy, and about Ellie Donovan. I came to tell you that if you said them again, I'd make you wish you was dead. But you *are* dead. You're a dead man on your feet, livin' in your own private hell. I couldn't make it any worse than this; I won't even try."

He turned his back on the judge and walked out the door.

Weary though he was, he couldn't sleep now. That unintentional nap broken up by Quince seemed to have taken the edge off. He lay tossing on his cot, trying to keep his eyes closed, knowing how bone-weary he was and how badly he needed rest. But through the night in a nightmarish half-sleep he kept seeing the rebellious face of Sandy Matlock. He could imagine Sandy riding beside Clabe Donovan, proud and straight in the saddle, taking the outlaw trail that once had come so near claiming Webb himself.

Webb rejected the picture. Once he heard himself cry out, "No!" He sat up on the edge of the cot and rubbed his face. He rummaged around in a bottom drawer of the desk for a bottle he had taken from a drunk and had forgotten to return later when the man was sober. He drank from it, shuddering at its bite but hoping it would drive away the image. It didn't. The picture was still there—Sandy and Donovan, side by side.

It didn't fit. It couldn't be . . . mustn't be! Sandy wasn't like that!

Webb finally dropped into a fitful sleep, awakening before sunup. He had to find out about Sandy, one way or the other. He went to Quince's livery stable. Quince was still sleeping soundly, snoring a little. The long ride had taken a lot out of Webb's old friend. Webb moved quietly to keep from waking him. He caught up a horse he sometimes borrowed and threw a saddle on him. Quince would know, when he saw Webb's saddle gone, that Webb had taken the animal. Before most of the town ever began to stir, Webb was on his way out toward Bronc Tomlin's Rafter T.

He knew he ought to have taken someone with him—Johnny Willet, perhaps, or even Quince. But this was a thing Webb had to do for himself. Sandy was *his* brother.

Hunger caught up with him, for he hadn't been eating much the last couple of days. As he rode, he ate from a can of sardines he had brought along, and drank from a can of tomatoes. When finally he reached the Rafter T headquarters, he didn't stop for a look around. He rode boldly up to the house. He shouted, "Bronc! Bronc Tomlin!"

He heard a movement and looked around to see a cowboy step up onto the little porch from somewhere around at one side of the house. It was the man named Clinch, the one Webb had surveyed so long from the hilltop near the cottonwood spring. Clinch still hadn't shaved. He slouched across to stop directly in front of Webb. "Bronc ain't here. Too bad."

"I've come to see him. Where's he at?"

"Gone off gatherin' horses. Won't be back for quite a while. You come again some other time."

Webb swung slowly down from the saddle. His hand close to his gun, he said firmly, "I reckon I'll go look for myself."

The cowboy stiffened. "Bronc give me orders to watch things. Ain't nobody goin' into that house without he says so."

"You better just step to one side, Clinch. I'm huntin' Bronc Tomlin, and I won't leave here till I've had a talk with him. You reach for that pistol and I'll have to use mine."

Webb dropped his reins and started toward the porch. The cowboy watched him indecisively, retreating a step. Just before Webb reached him, Clinch suddenly decided to act. He crouched and rushed. Webb stepped to one side, bringing up his pistol as he moved. He swung it and struck the barrel across the back of the cowboy's head. The felt hat cushioned the blow, but the man sprawled out flat on the ground, dazed. Webb reached down and took the pistol out of the cowboy's holster.

"Just to prevent temptation," he said. "Now I'm goin' in. I'd be much obliged if you wouldn't cause me no more trouble."

Half expecting Tomlin's bachelor house to smell as badly as the judge's did, he was a little surprised to find it well-aired and even to have a vague wisp of perfume about. He remembered then the saloon girl Bronc Tomlin had brought out from Rio Escondido. She was probably still here.

A closed door opened cautiously, and a frightened face looked out, a feminine face surrounded by long red hair that had missed a brushing.

Webb removed his hat. It was an old habit of his in the presence of women, and the fact that this was a saloon girl made no difference. "I'm lookin' for Bronc Tomlin," he said. "You got him in that room yonder?"

She shook her head, squinting for a better look at him. She must have seen Webb's badge, finally. The door opened wider, and she stepped into the front room. "You're a lawman? A Ranger or somethin'?"

"Sheriff."

She sighed in relief and moved toward him. She was not much over twenty, and she still had a pretty face. That face held a deep fear. "I didn't know if you'd find out, sheriff, but I'm sure glad you came. I want you to take me out of here."

"If I'd find out what?"

"Sheriff, he's not goin' to let me leave this place alive. I bribed a horse-breaker to take a note to town for me. Didn't you get it?"

Webb shook his head. "I didn't. Likely he just took your money and threw the note away."

"Money?" she said. Then she shrugged. "It doesn't matter, now that you're here. Please, just get me away from this godawful place."

Webb frowned. Maybe she knew a lot about what had happened—so much that Bronc Tomlin couldn't afford to let her get out of his hands. For a long time Webb had known to his own satisfaction that Tomlin was implicated with various border jumpers. He had never had enough proof to take action. Maybe this girl was what he needed to wrap Tomlin up tight.

"All right, Miss . . ."

"Smith. They just call me Blossom."

"Blossom, you get your things together. I'll take you to town."

She paused to look out the window worriedly. "I hope you're not by yourself."

"I am."

Some of the fear came back into her eyes. "Bronc Tomlin won't let us get away from here that easy. Not when you're just by yourself."

"I can handle Bronc Tomlin."

A voice spoke behind him. "Don't be making no bets, sheriff!"

Webb hadn't heard Tomlin ease up onto the porch. Now the man stood in the doorway, a gun in his hand. It wasn't pointed directly at Webb, but it wouldn't take Bronc the blinking of an eye to bring it up into line. The cowboy Webb had pistol-whipped stood behind Tomlin, peering over the horseman's shoulder. A thin trickle of blood had dried on the side of Clinch's face.

Tomlin said, "I got lots of patience, Matlock, but I don't like a man to abuse my hospitality. Clinch here told you I was gone. That ought to've been enough to satisfy you."

"But you weren't gone, Bronc. Not very far."

"If I'd of felt like visitin' with you, sheriff, I'd have come when I first saw you. I'm busy. Now you better just ride on back to town."

Webb watched Tomlin and weighed his chances of drawing his gun before Tomlin could shoot him. The chances weren't good.

"The young lady wants to go with me, Bronc. I'm takin' her."

Bronc shook his head. "I paid her to come out here awhile and keep house. She's goin' to stay."

Some housekeeper, Webb thought. "She'll go if she wants to."

Bronc's eyes narrowed. "She been tellin' you lies, sheriff? Man don't want to believe all these dancehall floozies tell him. They're great little liars, all of them, and this here gal is one of the best." He glared at the girl. "Now, you git ridin', sheriff. I don't want no trouble with you."

Webb Matlock stood his ground. He glanced at the trembling girl and saw desperation in her eyes. He said, "Bronc, I came here to find out somethin'. Did my brother Sandy ride with Clabe Donovan on that raid into Dry Fork?"

Blandly Tomlin said, "Raid? I don't know nothin' about no raid."

Grimly Webb replied, "You know plenty about that raid. I believe Sandy may have come back out here after I had that row with him. I want to know if you sent him ridin' with Donovan."

Tomlin shook his head. "Like I told you, I don't know nothin' about Donovan, or about no raid."

The girl cried, "That's a lie, sheriff. He knows all about it. Those outlaws were here, and they talked with him. He got a cut out of the money after it was all over."

Tomlin brought the gun up and trained it at Webb. But he cut a quick angry glance toward the girl. "Now you done it, Blossom. I never shot a woman in my life. I been tryin' hard to figure out some way to keep from havin' to shoot *you*. Now you've fixed it so I got to kill you *and* the sheriff."

Webb licked his dry lips. "Better think on it, Bronc. They won't hang you for bank robbery. They *will* hang you for murder."

"Not unless they find out. Now come on, sheriff, and slow.

You too, Blossom. I don't want to do this in the house. Clinch, get the sheriff's gun."

The cowboy said shakily, "God, Bronc, you really aim to do it?"

"I got no choice. I didn't want to."

"But a woman . . ."

"A dancehall girl, that's all. There won't nobody even miss her."

"Bronc, runnin' horses for a bunch of border jumpers is one thing. Killin' is somethin' else, especially a woman. You just check me out of this."

Webb saw a glimmer of hope. "You're too late, cowboy," he said. "Even if you leave now, you're mixed up in it. The truth'll come out, and they'll be after you with a rope."

The cowboy pleaded, "Bronc, we can leave them afoot and ride for the border. We can be across the river and safe before he can get halfway to town."

Bronc said, "You can run because you got nothin' to lose. All you own is the clothes on your back. I got this ranch and all my horses. I'm not givin' that up for a long-nosed sheriff and a two-bit wheeligo girl."

The girl sank to her knees. She cried, "Please, Bronc, please. I promise you I won't ever say a word, not a word."

"Too late for promises now. You ought to've thought of that when you was makin' threats. Now come on, or I'll have to do it right here."

She surrendered completely to her terror. She grabbed hold of a table leg and clung to it hysterically. "No! No!"

Her screaming made Webb's hair feel as if it were going to stand. It seemed to unnerve Bronc, too. This wasn't making a bad situation any better to him. Basically the man was not a killer, Webb knew. But in this case he had been forced into it against his will. For a second Bronc turned toward the girl, distracted. "Blossom . . ."

In that instant Webb took a wild chance. He dived headlong across the floor toward Bronc, grabbing at his gun. In reflex Tomlin whirled and pulled off a quick shot that splintered the floor almost where Webb had landed. Webb brought his pistol up and fired point blank just as Tomlin's hand tightened again. The slug hurled Bronc back against the wall. Bronc's fingers stiffened as he tried desperately to hold onto the gun. The pistol slipped free and clattered to the floor. Bronc slumped and lay gasping. The fabric smouldered where the close-fired bullet had burned through his shirt, just above the heart.

Webb rolled over onto his knees, smoking gun still in his hand. He trained it on the cowboy. "How about you, Clinch? You through?"

Clinch stared in shock, his hands shoulder high. "I didn't even start."

Webb said, "I ought to take you in, but I expect I'll have enough to worry about. You saddle up and ride out of here. Don't ever let me see your face in my county again."

Clinch nodded and started to back away. Then he paused. "Bronc owed me some wages."

"Take a good horse. That ought to even it up."

The cowboy left the porch in a strong trot.

Tomlin's shirt still smouldered. Webb touched it with his hand to put out the fire and found that Tomlin still lived. But he wouldn't for long.

"Bronc," Webb said quickly, "tell me now, before it's too late. Was Sandy with Donovan?"

Bronc coughed. He tried once to speak but couldn't. He took a short, painful breath.

Webb said, "Tell me, Bronc! Tell me!"

Bronc whispered, "Go to hell!" and he was dead.

From outside, Webb could hear a commotion. Through the open door he saw the handful of cowboys and Bronc riders who worked for Bronc. They were gathering in front of the porch. Clinch wasn't among them. He was probably already picking his horse and getting ready to ride. Webb stepped to the door and surveyed the group, looking for any threat. He saw none, but he held the pistol in his hand anyway.

"Boys," he said, "Bronc Tomlin is dead. I'll tell you what I told Clinch: saddle up and ride out. Don't ever come back or you'll wind up in jail. And don't ride south to Donovan, either. His day is about done."

Slowly the stunned men pulled away from the house and

headed toward the bunkhouse and the barn. In an hour or less, they would all be gone.

Webb had almost forgotten the girl. He turned to find her and saw that she had pulled herself to a chair at the table. She sat slumped over, her face buried in her arms. Her shoulders heaved. He could hear her quiet sobbing.

Sympathy moving in him, he touched her arm. Right now it didn't matter who she was or what she had been. She was simply a helpless young girl who had just gone through the most terrifying experience of her life.

"It's all over with," he said gently. "You'll live to be 90."

Regaining control of herself, she began trying to wipe the tears away with a handkerchief. Webb could see she was making a conscious effort not to look toward the still body of Bronc Tomlin.

"Thank you, sheriff. I'll tell you anything you want to know."

"With Bronc dead, a lot of what I was goin' to ask you won't matter now. What did he mean when he said you were makin' threats to him?"

"They sent a man with Bronc's share of the money. I told Bronc I wanted part of it for keepin' my mouth shut. That's how I made my mistake, gettin' greedy. I put him in a spot where he almost had to kill me." She pointed to a chest at the far side of the room. "That's where he put the money, sheriff. You can take it back to that bank."

Webb said, "Did you see Donovan?"

"No, he never did come by here himself, just sent messages. Bronc looked over the Rio Escondido bank for him. They even went so far as to set up a relay of horses for Donovan to use on his way back after robbin' the bank. But one of Bronc's boys was in Dry Fork when you and your posse pulled out. He headed Donovan off. Donovan decided not to go back to Mexico empty handed. With you and the town's best fightin' men gone anyway, he decided to take the Dry Fork bank instead."

Webb nodded. He had figured it had been something like that. He never had believed Donovan would go to all that trouble just to set up a ruse. Dry Fork had been a second choice, then, half a loaf taken instead of none.

The girl touched the handkerchief to her eyes. "You goin' to put me in jail, sheriff?"

He shook his head. "I don't see where it would help anybody. You did a wrong thing, but you came awful close to dyin' for it, and I don't expect you'll ever forget that. I'll see if I can rustle up a buckboard or somethin' to get you back to Dry Fork. Then, if you'll tell me all you know about Donovan, you'll be free to go wherever you want to."

Her chin stiffened. "I want to go home, sheriff. Back to my folks."

That sounded fine to him. "You sure?"

"I don't know why I ever left them. Stupid, I guess. It hasn't been an easy life, sheriff. I've done things and seen things . . ." She broke off a moment. "I'll live a clean life from now on, I promise you. I don't ever want to see another saloon."

Webb said, "That's fine, Blossom, sure fine. Now, just one more thing. You *did* see a few of Donovan's men. Was one of them young, about twenty-one, a good-lookin' kid with sandy-colored hair? They might've called him Sandy."

She thought hard, then slowly shook her head. "There were several young ones. A couple of them might have fit that description. I never did hear any names. Would you happen to have a picture?"

Disappointed, he said, "No, he never did go anywhere to have one made. We never were much for travelin'."

"Was he a partner of yours or somethin'?"

Webb said bleakly, "My brother!"

9

WEBB TOOK BLOSSOM SMITH TO DRY FORK IN BRONC Tomlin's buckboard. She studiously avoided looking at Bronc's body, blanket-wrapped in the back of the buckboard. The close brush with death had sobered her. Webb hoped she would stay sobered and live up to her vow to make a clean start.

Darkness came before they reached town. Webb was thankful for that. It should save him from having to make a lot of explanations, both about the girl and about Bronc Tomlin. He pulled up at the hotel and helped Blossom step down. The sleepy-eyed clerk waked up as he saw Blossom enter the small lobby. He looked her over from head to foot with obvious appreciation. He turned the register around to see what name she had signed. Taking a key from a hook, he spoke to Webb rather than to the girl.

"I'm givin' her room 16, sheriff. That's just down the hall."

Flushing a little, Webb said, "Tell her, not me."

The clerk shrugged, reappraising the situation. "Just thought maybe you'd want to know." He glanced at the girl. "Go ahead, miss. I'll bring your bags." The girl started down the short hall. As the clerk stooped to pick up the bags, Webb said, "Clarence, she tells me she wants to go clean. Don't you let anybody bother her."

He took the buckboard around to the back of the Hanks Mercantile and Hardware. Besides being the father of Sandy's girl friend, Birdie, Ashby Hanks was the town undertaker, such as there was. Selling hardware, it was only natural that he stock caskets. And stocking caskets, it was equally natural that he lay out the dead and prepare them for burial. One occupation seemed to fit in handily with the others. Webb knocked on the door of Hanks' adobe house. Birdie answered. Her eyes were red and swollen from crying.

"Hello, Webb," she said tightly.

He wished he could think of something to say to the sorrowing girl. He knew the anguish Birdie must be going through, defending Sandy when the town was condemning him. But what could a man say?

"I came to see your father, Birdie."

She turned half around and called, "Dad!" Then to Webb, "Any news about Sandy?"

He lowered his chin. "None. I'm sorry, Birdie."

"He didn't do it, Webb," she said fiercely. "One day they'll all find out they were wrong." He saw a stubborn faith burning in the girl's eyes and wished he had it himself.

"I'm glad you believe in him, Birdie," he said.

Hanks had been relaxing in his sock feet. He came to the door, his shoes still untied. Webb said, "I'm afraid I got a customer for you, Ashby."

"Kind of late, sheriff, but I'm always pleased to wait on a customer."

Webb shook his head. "Not one like this. He won't ever be back." He turned and walked to the buckboard. Webb lifted a corner of the blanket so Hank could see Bronc. Tomlin's face.

Hanks swallowed and asked, "How?"

Webb told him briefly what had happened. They carried Bronc into a small room at the back of Hanks' store, a room kept for just that purpose. They placed the body on a board. Hanks stepped back and gazed at it pensively. "Can't say I ever liked Bronc Tomlin much, but on the other hand it's hard to hold much reproach for a man when you see him like this. Makes you feel a little sad, somehow, no matter who he was or what he did."

Hanks began to roll up his sleeves. "Second time today I've had to do this job, Webb. Reckon you left town too early to know."

Surprised, Webb asked quickly, "Who died?"

"Judge Upshaw. Hanged himself, the judge did. Got so afraid Donovan was going to kill him that he just went and did it himself. Dutchman went over this morning to take the judge his breakfast. Found him hanging there. Empty whisky bottle on the floor. Judge must have drunk it all before he did the job."

Regret touched Webb, and he stared at the floor. This was a sorry way for any man to go. "I went over there and talked to him last night. I could tell he was in despair. It never occurred to me he would take that way out."

Hanks shrugged. "He wasn't the bravest man in the world, the judge."

Webb clenched his fist and stared out the open door into the darkness beyond the lamplight. "Donovan! Those he doesn't kill for himself, he reaches somehow else. One way or another, he gets them."

Webb wouldn't have expected to have any appetite after all that had happened today, but he found himself hungry. He hadn't eaten much lately. Out of long habit he walked down to Ellie Donovan's cafe without intending to. From the shadows he looked through the windows at Ellie. He stood and watched her and wished. Then he walked on to the Dutchman's for supper.

It was a dismal meal because the Dutchman insisted on giving him all the grim details of how he had come to find the judge. He didn't leave out a thing, so far as Webb could tell.

About the time Webb finished eating, Johnny Willet found him. Webb was thankful for the deputy's arrival because it shut the Dutchman up. Johnny drank a cup of black coffee while Webb finished his meal and smoked a cigarette. The two had little more than "Howdy" to say to each other. Finished, they walked out on the street together. Then Webb told him what had happened at Bronc Tomlin's.

Johnny asked, "Figured out what you're goin' to do next, Webb?"

Webb nodded somberly. "The only thing I *can* do, Johnny. We can't just let this thing run on forever. I'm goin' down and get Donovan!"

"But he's across the river."

"I'll go across the river too."

Johnny chewed his lip. "You remember what happened the last time we swam the *rio?*"

"I remember. But that time we had a whole posse along, and we got stopped before our feet were even dry. A couple or three men, though, might slip across at night and not arouse too much suspicion."

"When do we leave, Webb?"

"We? I hadn't even asked you, Johnny."

"You don't have to ask. I'm goin'. You got anybody else in mind?"

Webb said, "One more, maybe. The big hitch is that we don't really have any clear idea where to look for Donovan. I thought I'd see Florentino Rodriguez. We might come up needin' a good tracker."

Johnny thoughtfully rubbed his chin. He glanced at Webb as if afraid Webb would take exception to the proposal Johnny was about to make. But Johnny made it anyway. "Maybe we wouldn't have to go there plumb blind. There's one person in town who might give us a good idea where to hunt."

Webb glanced sharply at Johnny. "You talkin' about Ellie?"

Johnny said defensively, "She *is* his wife. She knows the habits he used to have. Ain't likely he's changed them a lot. She could tell us, if she wanted to."

Webb said, "Johnny, I already asked her once. Like you said, she is his wife. It isn't fair to ask her again."

"Maybe this time she would see it different."

Adamant, Webb shook his head. "No, Johnny. I won't ask her."

He walked down into the south part of the settlement and made his way to Florentino's adobe. As he neared the door, he could hear Consuela Rodriguez softly singing a Mexican lullaby. He saw her in an old rocking chair, swaying forward and back, putting the new baby to sleep. Webb said quietly, "Florentino?"

Florentino appeared in the lamplighted doorway, squinting cautiously out into the darkness. He held a gun, but it was not in a position where he could readily have used it if Donovan had been waiting for him.

"It's just me," Webb said. "Can I talk to you?"

"Come in," Florentino said softly, looking toward the baby. Consuela found the child was asleep. She arose carefully and placed it in a handmade wooden cradle. Webb stepped over to look at the child. It's sleepy face was round and brown and totally at peace.

Webb said, "I'd give a lot to be able to sleep that way. No worries bearin' down—just lie there and sleep and let the world go by."

Florentino said wistfully in Spanish, "Only a child can do it. Once a person grows up and loses peace, it is gone forever."

Webb observed, "The baby is pretty. Favors you, Mrs. Rodriguez." Slow with English, Consuela had to have a translation from Florentino. Webb shifted to Spanish, "I'm afraid I didn't come to look at the baby, Florentino. I came to tell you I'm going across the river after Donovan."

Florentino frowned. "You came to ask me to go with you?"

"I'm not asking you anything. I thought you would want to know when I went."

"But you would like to have me?"

Webb nodded. "We don't really know where to start looking for him. We may need a good tracker."

Consuela's eyes widened in anxiety. She warned, "Florentino, it is dangerous. Remember Aparicio."

Florentino cut her off with a wave of his hand. "I *am* remembering Aparicio." In Mexican families the woman was expected to accept the man's decisions without question or doubt. Often it didn't really turn out that way, but she was usually discreet enough not to argue with him in the presence of outsiders and cause him to lose stature.

Florentino stared down a while at his new son. "How many will go?"

"Just Johnny Willet and me. And you, if you decide to. It isn't many, but a big posse couldn't slip across that river. Three men might."

Memories kindled an anger that darkened Florentino's face. "I have much to settle with Donovan. This bad leg of mine, for one thing. Aparicio, for another. Except for Donovan, Aparicio would be alive and with us tonight." He looked at the baby. "Last time the child was due, and I would not go. Now my son is here, and there is nothing to hold me. Get a horse for me, Mister Webb. I will go with you."

Consuela Rodriguez voiced no protest. She turned away, her head down, and silently made the sign of the cross.

Returning, Webb walked by Jake Scully's saloon. He heard a woman's laughter and stopped in surprise. Women were rarely seen in Jake's. The town's "good" women usually moved to the edge of the street or even crossed over when they passed. As for saloon girls, Jake never hired them. He had strong moral feelings, in his own fashion, and he kept his place strictly a man's establishment. A man went there to drink, gamble, or talk. If he wanted anything else, he went to some other place.

Peering inside, Webb swore softly. Perched on the edge of a table was Blossom Smith, her long dress pulled up just enough to show her trim ankles and high-laced shoes. Men had drawn chairs into a semi-circle around her. Jake Scully, usually on the grumpy side, looked dangerously close to smiling as he eyed the girl and the rapidly-emptying glasses in the hands of the men. He saw Webb and gave him a nod, inviting him in.

Frowning, Webb pointed his chin at the girl. "What's she doin' here?"

"She's doublin' business, is what she's doin'. I got no idea who she is. She just come a-wanderin' in here while ago. Draws men like honey draws flies."

"You don't usually allow this kind of thing, Jake."

"She ain't done nothin' shady, if that's what you mean. Minute she does, I'll tell her to go."

Webb watched the girl. His first reaction was anger and disappointment in her. But he could see the happy shine in her eyes, and he realized she was in her true element. She did this because she wanted to, and no amount of moralizing would change that. All her talk of reformation had gone for naught, a passing fancy born of fear and quickly forgotten.

Webb shrugged, a sense of frustration touching him, then fading. "You know, Jake, everybody has his own ways. You can't make one person be like somebody else. You try to change people, but you find they won't make themselves over into what you want them to be. You have to accept people the way they are."

Jake nodded, though he had only the foggiest notion what Webb was talking about.

Webb asked, "You goin' to let her stay here, Jake?"

"I'm not hirin' her. But as long as she keeps them turnin' their glasses up and don't take none of them out the back door, I don't reckon I'll run her off."

On his way back to the office, Webb noticed that Ellie Donovan's cafe was closed and dark. On impulse he stopped and looked toward her house. Maybe before he left he should tell her . . . But the house was dark, and he knew he shouldn't try to see her anyway. Getting so it was an ordeal for them both.

He stopped on the office porch to look back down the street and roll a cigarette. He stood there drawing thoughtfully upon the smoke, thinking ahead, wondering what would happen down yonder across the river.

He heard a movement inside the office and spun around,

hand dropping instinctively to the gun at his hip. Dread gripped him, for ambush had become Donovan's way.

Ellie Donovan's voice came from the darkness of the room. "Webb, I came to talk to you."

"Ellie!" He swallowed, his heart pounding from the surprise.

She said, "I didn't intend to scare you."

"You didn't, exactly. It's just that here lately . . ." His hand flexed nervously, and he wiped cold sweat onto his pants leg. "I never expected to see you here, Ellie."

"I never expected to have to come here. But I'm told you're going after Clabe."

Webb peered toward her intently, wishing he could see her better in the darkness. "How did you hear that? I been keepin' it quiet."

"Johnny Willet came and told me. He said you wouldn't ask me to help you."

With a sudden impatience, Webb said, "No, I wouldn't, and he had no right to ask you either."

"He didn't ask me, Webb. He just said he thought I had a right to know what you were planning. And I think I do have such a right, Webb. Not only because of what Clabe used to mean to me, but because of what you have been to me, too."

"I wish you hadn't found out, Ellie. Knowin' won't help you any. It'll just cause you pain."

"There's pain either way."

He pulled on the cigarette, fist drawn tight. "It's been tough on you, Ellie. If I had my way . . ."

Abruptly she said, "I'm going with you, Webb!"

He dropped the cigarette. "Ellie . . ."

She didn't give him time to begin arguing. "Webb, you asked me once if I would tell you where you might be most likely to find Clabe. I said I couldn't do that to him because he was my husband. I still felt that much loyalty to him. Now I've changed my mind. People have died because of him, and even this town has begun to die a little. There is fear in the people here.

"He's done something to you too, Webb. You've changed

since he came back. And there's that matter about Sandy. Some people have even hinted that you've held back on Clabe because of me, that you're in love with me and afraid that if you bring Clabe in you'll lose me. It's not fair to you to keep letting them point fingers. So I'm going with you, Webb."

"You can't, Ellie. No tellin' what we might run into."

"Without me you won't have any idea where to start."

"You could tell us. That would be enough."

"It's been too many years ago, Webb. I could find it myself, but I could never tell anybody else how to. The only way is for me to go." She placed her hand on his arm. "Please, Webb, I have to go."

Still doubtful, Webb took hold of her hand. "You know what's likely to happen if we find him. Are you prepared to be a witness to it?"

She leaned toward him, her face against his chest. "I know, Webb, but I've let it go too far already. It's time now to stop him, even if he is still my husband."

"And even though you still love him?"

For a minute she stood in silence, leaning against him. He reached up to touch her cheek and found it wet with tears. She whispered, "Even though I still love him!"

10

LONG BEFORE DAYLIGHT THEY MET IN QUINCE PYBURN'S livery barn and saddled their horses by lanternlight behind the closed doors. The fewer people who knew about this, the better. There would be that much less chance of word somehow getting to Clabe Donovan.

Quince finished lashing down a pack over a fifth horse which was to be led. Then he rechecked the sidesaddle on Ellie's horse and complained because Webb wouldn't let him go.

Webb said, "Every extra man and horse we take cuts our chance of gettin' by."

"But just three men . . ."

"We don't aim to take on an army. We'll find out where Clabe is, sneak in and grab him, then run like hell."

"Supposin' he ain't keen on comin' along?"

Webb glanced at Ellie Donovan and refrained from making an answer. The answer was plain enough even unspoken.

Quince said, "You-all have a lot of guts to try this, especially after what happened the other time. I only wish I could go with you. I still got a feelin' you'll be a-wishin' you had help." His gaze went back to Ellie, his eyes soft. "The most courageous one is you, Ellie. In your place, I couldn't do it."

Ellie dropped her chin and blinked quickly. Quince said, "It ain't too late. You could still back out."

She said, "Give me a boost up, will you, Quince?"

Gently he gave her a footlift to help her onto the saddle. Webb raised the bar that blocked the back door and led his horse outside. He opened the one remaining corral gate. In the east he could see the beginnings of daylight. Somewhere out behind Quince's haystack a rooster saw it, too, and proclaimed it with all the pride of his calling. Before long, people would be up and stirring. They arose early in a country town like this. Webb mounted and made a forward motion with his hand. Johnny Willet took the packhorse's lead rope from Quince. The horse was saddled, the pack tied down across the saddle. That would be for Clabe Donovan to ride . . . if they took him alive.

Eyes worried, Quince said, *"Buena suerte."*

"Thanks, Quince," Webb replied. "We'll need that luck."

They left Dry Fork, jog-trotting to put some distance behind them early. Later Webb slacked the pace because he knew the ride was going to be hard enough on Ellie even as it was. She hadn't been a-horseback much the last few years. They rode slowly because there was no need for haste, now that they were well clear of town. They would reach the river considerably before dark anyway, and they couldn't afford a daylight crossing. They would save the horses' strength for a time when it might be needed more.

Johnny Willet said, "Webb, mind if I make a suggestion?"

Webb hadn't said much to Johnny, for he had been angry with him for speaking to Ellie. Now the anger was gone. Webb was actually glad Ellie had been told, for it meant a better chance of finding Clabe Donovan.

"This isn't an army outfit, Johnny. Any suggestions are welcome."

"I've ridden up and down that river so many times lately that I know it pretty good. I know where there's a big gravel bar leadin' up on the Mexico side. Hoof tracks wouldn't show much if we crossed there. With a little luck, that bunch of Mexican horse cavalry wouldn't even see them."

"Sounds good to me," Webb said.

Late in the afternoon they came to a place where the land suddenly broke away before them into a chalky *guajilla* ridge. Beyond that, partially screened by a heavy stand of mesquite brush and catclaw, the surface of the river reflected the sun with a sparkling sheen that seemed to deny the ugly muddiness of it. Webb drew rein to keep from standing out against the skyline, where he might easily be spotted by anyone who happened to be across the river. He pulled back into the cover of the brush.

Johnny Willet said in satisfaction, "We hit it pretty good. That gravel bar ain't but a little ways upstream."

Florentino Rodriguez's eyes glittered with a grim resolve. He hadn't said much today. Now he asked evenly, "How far to where they shoot Aparicio?"

Johnny Willet looked westward. "Four or five miles. Pretty muddy on the Mexico side at that point. We'd leave tracks a foot deep."

Webb said, "It wouldn't help anything for you to see the place."

The Mexican shook his head. "It is not so important where Aparicio dies. It is important who kill him."

Webb turned his horse away from the river. "We'd best ease off a ways and find us a shady place to wait for night. We need to rest some anyway and cook supper before sundown so we can have the fire out by dark."

Not far from the river they found a few ancient, gnarled old liveoak trees growing along a near-dry creek that fed into the Rio. In the deep shade and the soft mat of rotted old leaves, they unsaddled and staked the horses at the ends of their ropes to graze. Ellie dug into the pack they had removed from the led horse. She began preparing supper.

Webb stood for a moment and stared at her. Ellie's face was dusty from the long ride, and dark lines beneath her eyes showed how tired she was. Probably hadn't slept last night, worrying about today and what was yet to come.

"Lie down and rest a while, Ellie," he said. "I'll take care of supper."

"Cooking is my job. I'll do it."

Probably wanted to keep busy, he thought. Couldn't say he blamed her. "I'll start a fire, then." He kindled a small blaze, took the coffee pot and fetched water from the creek.

"Water's not the clearest I ever saw, but I reckon the coffee will cover up the mud."

They took their time eating supper and washing the utensils they had used. The fire had died down to embers; just enough to keep the coffee pot hot, and it was well hidden by the banks of the winding creek. Dusk came. This river country was at a lower altitude than Webb was used to at Dry Fork, and the daytime heat was oppressive. Now, with evening, the heat slowly gave way to a cool breeze drifting north from Mexico.

Ellie had spread a blanket on the soft cover of old leaves at the base of a liveoak tree so that she might lie down and rest. But she wasn't lying down. She sat with her knees drawn up under her chin, the long skirt spread out around her so that not even her feet were showing. She stared sadly into the darkness, immersed in thought, oblivious to everything around her.

Webb watched her a long time but left her alone until finally he saw her chin drop, her hands covering her face. He walked over to her.

"Ellie, you don't have to do it. Nobody would blame you if you decided to turn around now and go back to Dry Fork."

She looked up, but not at Webb. She kept staring off into the night. "I feel like some kind of a Judas. I'm betraying him. All the talk in the world won't change that."

"You haven't betrayed him. If you want to go home . . ."

"Want to? You know how much I want to. But I owe as much to the people of Dry Fork as I ever owed to Clabe. More, maybe. He has become a curse to the people who are my friends. Now, whichever way I go, I'm betraying somebody—either Clabe or my friends."

"You're not to blame, Ellie. There's no part of it that's your own doing."

"That doesn't make it any easier."

Webb touched her hand, then pulled back. His heart went out to her. But all he could do was hold his distance and look at the ground and endure the ache of denial.

"Whichever you decide, Ellie, I'll stand behind you all the way."

Her voice was unexpectedly firm. "I've already decided, Webb. I decided last night."

In the dark time before the rising of the moon they reined into the cool water and pointed their horses' heads toward the bar of gravel on the south side of the Rio. Webb rode close beside Ellie, ready to grab her if her horse had any trouble in the deep part of the river. They moved slowly, trying to make no more noise than they had to. There might not be a human being within miles on either side of the river. But again, the Mexican officer Armendariz and his patrol might be camped anywhere.

Halfway across, Ellie's horse began to flounder. The ground had dropped away from beneath his feet. Webb pulled in quickly and grabbed Ellie around the waist. She dropped the reins and threw both arms around his neck. The horse went under, splashing, but Webb pulled Ellie against him and held her tightly. His own horse never wavered. Soon Webb's dun found good footing and waded up onto the gravel bar. The river lay behind them, murmuring quietly. But for a long moment Webb continued to hold Ellie, and she held onto him. Not intending to, he kissed her, and her own arms seemed to tighten around him.

"Oh, Webb," she whispered, "Webb."

"It's all right now, Ellie," he said. "It's all right."

Gently he eased her to the ground. He swung off the horse and caught her hand again. "Scare you?"

She nodded, and he found she was shaking a little. "A bit, not bad. It's over now." She pulled her hand away and bowed her head. "Or maybe it's just started."

Johnny and Florentino brought back Ellie's horse. It was dancing around in eye-rolling panic, water running out of its mane and tail, dripping from its body. Florentino stepped down and began to pat the horse's neck, speaking soft Spanish in an effort to calm it down.

Webb said, "We better get off this bar and out of sight. Moon'll come up directly, and this gravel will shine."

They moved afoot into the cover of brush 50 yards from

the river. It was the same brush one found on the Texas side, the same air. He heard the same birds singing. Hard to believe that short swim had put them into a different country. A different country, an alien land where he was no longer an officer of the law. Rather, he was here against the law. He reached down and unpinned the sheriff's badge from his shirt. He rubbed his fingers over it a moment, then shoved it into his pocket.

"Badge won't mean anything over here," he said, more to himself than to anyone. "Might even make matters worse, if things go wrong."

The moon was beginning to rise. Looking back, the way the moonlight slanted across the gravel bar, Webb could see that the horses' hoofs had left pocks that showed patches of shadow. Johnny Willet saw them too. He broke a limb from a dead mesquite and walked back to the water's edge. He began raking over the gravel, smoothing out the pocks.

He was almost through when a Spanish voice cried, *"Quién es?"* Who is it? *"Qué pasa aquí?"* What's going on here?

The voice came from somewhere ahead, in the edge of the brush. Webb realized that Ellie had walked on in front, leading her horse. He drew his gun and sprinted toward her, his breath short from the sudden surprise. Ellie stood startled, her hand over her mouth. Webb put his arm around her and gently pushed her back. He had the pistol up and ready.

Then he saw they had walked into a small camp set up by an old Mexican man and a little boy. Dying embers glowed in what was left of a campfire, almost smothered now in ashes. The man stood uncertainly, his eyes large. The frightened little boy clung to the man's leg. A couple of fishing poles rested against a mesquite where a droop-eared burro was tied. Swallowing hard, Webb lowered the gun, then let it drop back into the holster.

The old man said in frightened Spanish, "We have nothing worth your stealing. We have no money."

Florentino Rodriguez made a gesture for the old man to sit down if he wished. "We do not come to harm you. We did not even know you were here. Do not be afraid of us."

The old man seemed slowly to decide Florentino was telling the truth. He began to relax. Finally he said, "We would
offer you food, but we have none. The few fish we caught,
we have already eaten."

Webb said, "We have had our supper. We are riding on."
He frowned. "Have you seen anything of the Mexican cavalry patrol?"

A touch of fear came back into the old man's voice. "You
are friends of Armendariz?"

Webb could tell that the *viejo* was not. "We are not
friends. We want to be sure we do not come across him."

"*Bueno*. A while before dark he came with six of his men.
They went down the river. They are probably camped at the
home of the Gonzales family."

"How do you know?"

"This Gonzales, he has a young daughter. The lieutenant
has a liking for girls."

"And Gonzales does not object?"

"No one can object to what Armendariz does. He has
killed men who tried. There is hardly a village on the river
that cannot show you the graves of men the lieutenant has
killed. Even a woman or two."

Webb glanced at the clouding face of Florentino. He said,
"There is at least one grave on the other side of the river,
too."

Florentino said tightly, "It is time this Armendariz fills a
grave of his own."

Sternly Webb reminded, "Florentino, we came after Clabe
Donovan. That has got to be first."

Florentino clenched his fists. Regretfully he said, "I
know."

"Providence has a way of takin' care of men like Armendariz."

Florentino turned toward his horse. "Providence is slow.
Sometimes it is hard to wait."

Johnny Willet brought Ellie's horse. The animal had settled down now. Most of its fright was gone, although it might
take a struggle to get the horse back into that river.

Ellie asked the old Mexican in broken Spanish, "Is this

the right direction to the village of San Miguel, the one at the edge of the Rancho Villareal?"

The old man nodded. "*Si*, but a little more to the west. You have been there before?"

"Years ago."

"It has not changed much. It is no bigger, and a little the poorer."

Webb's eyebrows raised. "San Miguel?" He had never heard of it. But there were dozens of such tiny villages, virtually unknown except by those who lived there. "Is that where you think Clabe will be?"

She nodded gravely. "I think so. It is where we lived. We had a house at the edge of the village. It looked down on a pretty valley of little fields and green meadows where the cattle grazed. Clabe loved it there, Webb. He was not all bad then. No man could be all bad who could have so much love for a place. He used to say that someday when we had gotten all the money we needed we would go far away and try to find another place just like it. I would tell him we didn't need money, and we didn't need to go anywhere else. We had the perfect place right there, at the village of San Miguel. Times I thought he was about ready to agree with me, that he would quit the things he was doing. He did love that place. That is why now I think he would be there again."

"I guess the village has some wonderful memories for you, Ellie. It's a shame to have to go there now and spoil it."

She shook her head. "It was spoiled years ago. That was why I left. I realized he never would change. I knew someday he would ride out and not come back. Every time he did come back, I thanked God he was still alive, and yet I knew he had blood on his hands. I came to hate the village, the whole valley. I thought I even hated Clabe. You know how close hate and love can be. Finally I ran. It was all I could do, just as now this is the only thing I can do."

Webb placed his hand on her shoulder. "And we'd better be movin'. I want to get away from this river a few miles before we stop to rest." He gave her a footlift and helped her onto the sidesaddle. Her skirts were still wet from the crossing.

Florentino said to the old man, "*Por favor, amigo*, if anyone asks, you have not seen us."

The *viejo* shook his head. "We have seen nothing and heard nothing."

"*Bueno*. Good fishing."

"Go with God."

They were four or five miles south and west of the river when Webb took his pocketwatch and slanted it toward the moon to see the dial. "Well past midnight," he said. "I reckon we better rest."

"I am not tired," Ellie said.

"We got to think of the horses. We may be ridin' a right smart faster comin' back than we are goin' in."

In a dry grassy draw he found a spot where Ellie could spread her blanket and lie down in relative comfort. The three men moved away a short distance to afford her some privacy. Webb did not try to set up a guard shift. He thought it unlikely that anyone would ride up on them at this hour. Even if they did, he was a light sleeper. It didn't take much to bring him to his feet, wide awake.

He didn't really expect to sleep much, but several sleepless nights were catching up with him. He dropped off and didn't wake up until the rising sun caught him in the face. He sat up quickly, blinking in surprise. For a few seconds he didn't remember where he was.

The morning air was cool and fresh. The staked horses were beginning to move around a little, cropping the curing grass. Webb gathered some dry wood and kindled a fire. By the time he had filled the coffee pot out of his and Johnny's canteens, Johnny and Florentino were up and around. Breakfast wouldn't amount to much except a little fried bacon and some cold biscuits. But the coffee had a good smell. It brought Ellie up. She came with her blanket rolled under her arm. Her face was showing some burn from yesterday's sun, and dust still clung to it. But her hair was freshly brushed. Even out this way, a woman remained a woman, and Webb was glad for it.

They ate and rode on as the sun began rising and building its heat in the cloudless east. With the passing hours they moved across a changing land, a thirsty land of mesquite and catclaw, chaparral and huisache, and prickly pear that stood hip high to a tall man, its spring blossoms long since burned away by the hot sun but still leaving a clinging remnant like black ashes.

Stopping on the crest of a hill, Webb made a sweeping motion with his hand. "Any of this look familiar to you, Ellie?"

She took her time. Finally she shook her head. "It's been a long time, Webb. Maybe a little farther on . . ."

About noon they came to a small creek, with a tumbled-down adobe house standing back a hundred feet from its sloping bank. In front of the house, their roots feeding from the soft mud of the creek, was a row of apple trees, alien to this dry land. The adobe hadn't been inhabited for some time, but it was obvious that this place was a favorite of travelers. A well-defined trail led to it and away again.

"I know this place," Ellie said suddenly. "At least, I think I do. A family lived here. Menchaca, I think their name was." They rode in so she could have a better look. The more she looked, the surer she became. "I passed by here when I was running from Clabe. These people fed me, I wonder why they left?"

Looking at the slope that climbed behind the house, Webb said, "I think I can see the reason." He rode up and looked at a mound and a cross. The paint was fading, and he could not decipher the date. But he could make out the words in Spanish:

Adolfo Menchaca, age 37. Murdered by Armendariz.

Webb's face twisted. "Armendariz. He's been busy."

Johnny Willet picked a few ripe apples and washed them in the creek. He carried one to Ellie. She looked at the cross and shook her head. "I don't know—I'd feel a little bad about it."

"These folks fed you the other time," Johnny pointed out. "I'll bet they'd want you to have some of their apples."

Ellie took one, rubbed it in her hands and bit into it. Her

face lighted a little and she said, "Good." Then she began looking around again. A melancholy came over her. "They seemed like good people, happy people. Not the kind who would ever bother anybody."

Webb said, "It's usually the innocent who get hurt when a mad dog runs loose."

Ellie flinched. Webb realized how that must have sounded to her. "Ellie, I didn't go to hurt you."

She shook her head. "You didn't say anything that wasn't true. Let's leave this place."

The farther they rode, the more familiar the land became to her. Now she was retracing the tracks she had left years ago. She had some difficulty because the last time she saw it as she rode north, and it was natural that some of the landmarks appeared different when viewed from the opposite side.

At mid-afternoon Ellie drew up, her face tense. "Webb, I think when we cross the next hill we'll see it—the valley of San Miguel."

Webb considered the hill. "Not much brush cover up there. We better get off and walk as we get near the top. We won't stand as tall thataway."

They circled, moving around the sloping side of the hill rather than directly across the top of it. Webb watched Ellie with concern. She was dragging her feet wearily. She walked with her mouth open, breathing hard. For her sake, he hoped this search wouldn't take much longer. But even if it didn't, there would still be the ride out. Well, he philosophized, one did what had to be done. Before the mission was finished, she might prove as strong as the men were. Often a woman had more endurance than a man when stress demanded it. He thought Ellie Donovan was that kind of woman. She had endured much in recent years.

They moved down below the crest of the hill before they stopped. Ellie stared at the little valley which lay like an oasis in an irregular pattern along a winding creek. Her lips were tight.

"That's the one, Webb. That village is San Miguel!"

11

IT WAS HARDLY A TOWN. EVEN THE SMALLEST OF MEXICAN villages was likely to boast a central *plaza* or square. This one didn't. San Miguel was really only a loose scattering of adobe houses, spaced out in an irregular manner along the creek which through countless centuries had built a fine-loam soil from the leavings of floodwaters sweeping down from the desert country around. Now this valley, small though it was, furnished sustenance for a number of families. It grazed their livestock and yielded small but fertile gardens which the people watered by means of small *acequias*, irrigation canals, zigzagging out from the creek.

Ellie pointed. Her voice was strained. "Yonder is our house, Clabe's and mine. Clabe bought it from the family which had built it. He could have just moved in and taken over, because these people aren't fighters. But he paid for it, Webb. He wasn't really a bad man, then."

The house was built a little higher off the creek than were most of the others. Webb thought it probably would give a good view over most of the valley. That would have been one reason Clabe Donovan liked it so much. "A good place for a man who wanted to get himself lost," he observed aloud. "It's not a place a posse would be apt to come across by accident. They'd have to know where it was."

Johnny Willet said, "Not much of a place for a man who

liked to have a good time, I'll bet. Don't look like there's even as much as a *cantina*."

Ellie said, "Clabe never did go for that sort of thing much. Some of his men did. There's a bigger village named Arroyo de Lopez about twenty miles from here. They used to go there and spend most of their time. Clabe seldom went there except to round them up."

Webb felt a prickling of excitement. "If he hasn't changed, then, he's likely to be down around that house right now. And most of his men could be over at that other town, Arroyo de Lopez."

Ellie nodded, her eyes downcast. "Could be."

The main problem as Webb saw it was that the adobe lay on the other side of the creek. To avoid the danger of being seen they had to ride far up the creek, cross over, circle way around and come in behind the place. To cross now in plain view would either flush the quarry or put him ready for a fight, depending upon how strong he might be.

Webb could see guilt and apprehension in Ellie's sad face. "Ellie," he said, "why don't you stay here? When it's all over, you can come on in."

She considered a moment. "I've come this far. I'll go the whole way."

"It may not be pleasant."

"It hasn't been, so far. I'm ready whenever you are."

It took them well over an hour to make the circle a-horseback. They stepped off their horses in a thicket a couple of hundred yards from the adobe. They looped their reins over branches. Turning away from Ellie in hopes she wouldn't notice, Webb drew his pistol and checked it. But he knew she had seen. Her shoulders were hunched in dread.

"Ellie," he said, "this time you've got to stay put. This is as far as you go. If Clabe's here . . ."

She nodded in resignation. "I won't argue with you. I'll stay here."

He turned to go. She said, "Webb . . ." He found her looking at him with tears in her eyes. "Webb, I just want you to know . . . I won't blame you for anything. But please, try not to kill him."

"I'll try," he promised.

He led the way, Johnny Willet hurrying to catch up with him, Florentino limping along behind, moving as fast as his stiff leg would allow him. Webb gripped his pistol. Johnny carried the short rifle from his saddle scabbard. Florentino, not particularly a good marksman, had a shotgun. If a man got close enough with one of those, he didn't have to be good.

They moved as near the house as they could without getting out of the mesquite and its covering foliage. Webb dropped to his stomach and studied the place. Johnny and Florentino knelt beside him.

"Somebody's been usin' the place," Webb observed. "See how the ground is packed? Horse tracks around it. I smell woodsmoke too. I expect somebody cooked dinner here."

They watched for a time but saw no sign of movement around the house. Down in the valley a Mexican worked a garden, and a small boy on a burro was driving a couple of cows.

Webb wished he could tell more about the place. It could be empty, or it could hold half a dozen of Clabe Donovan's outlaws. "We're about as close as we can get without steppin' out into the open. I say to shoot the works, make a dash for the house. It's liable to come as such a surprise to them that they can't get a shot at us till we're flat against the walls. Then they can't get out without comin' past us."

He glanced at the Mexican. "On second thought, Florentino, maybe you better stay here. That bad leg is goin' to slow you down—keep you in the open too long. You can cover us from here."

Florentino accepted Webb's logic. "This shotgun, it don't do much so far away."

Johnny traded with him, giving Florentino the rifle.

Webb said, "Let's go."

They sprinted into the open. As he ran, Webb tried to watch the windows. With luck nobody would be looking.

The 50 yards hadn't appeared far before. Now that he was in it and running, it looked like a mile to the house. He wasn't used to running this way. The high heels didn't help.

Still he saw no movement at the window. This was just too much luck . . . too much luck . . .

He made it to the wall and flattened against it, half expecting a shot to be fired even yet. Johnny reached the wall only a step behind him. They stood with backs against the rough, plaster-shedding adobe, breathing hard from the long run. Webb's heart beat heavily, and not altogether from the exercise. His mouth was dry.

He listened for movement, but these adobe houses with thick mud walls and dirt floors carried little sound.

They must have made it unseen, he figured. If they had been spotted, someone inside the house would have made a move by now. Webb motioned for Johnny to circle the house from the other side. They met at the front, still keeping themselves flat against the wall. They dared not speak. Webb hardly even dared breathe. Carefully he crept toward the door. He made sign talk to Johnny.

Inside. Me first, then you.

He took a deep breath, bracing himself. Then he leaped through the door. He saw a sudden movement near a corner of the room. Heart in his throat, he swung the gun around, finger tensed on the trigger.

He was prepared for anything but what he saw.

A young Mexican woman sat on a straight rawhide chair, rocking her body back and forth to put a baby to sleep. On a rough blanket spread upon the earthen floor lay a girl two or three years old, already asleep.

Webb heard Johnny vault into the room behind him. The woman had stared in terrified silence at Webb. Now, at sight of Johnny she screamed. The baby jerked in her arms and began to cry. The little girl rose up on the pallet, eyes big in fright. She saw the guns and began to wail.

"Dónde está Donovan?" Webb demanded. *Where is Donovan?*

The woman trembled, frightened too badly to speak. She shrank back from the men, even after they holstered their guns to reassure her.

"We do not come to harm you," Webb told her in her own

language. "Do not be afraid of us. We have come to find the man Donovan."

"There is no Donovan here," she managed. Then she broke down in fright and began to sob. Both of her children were crying too. It was something of a bedlam. Webb began backing toward the door, realizing he had upset a household for no valid reason. He glanced at Johnny and saw astonishment in the young cowboy's eyes.

"Looks like we just muddied the water," Webb said. "And the fish all gone."

He stepped outside and hailed Florentino. Webb stood in the open, his hands empty, to let the Mexican know the coast was clear. Florentino came in a run that was half hop, favoring the bad leg.

Florentino halted, breathing hard. "The place is empty?"

"Not quite. Listen."

Florentino's face twisted in confusion as he listened to the children's crying. "That is not Donovan."

Webb shook his head. "You can talk to the woman better than I can. See if you can find out what's happened here."

By the time they got the young woman calmed down, Ellie Donovan came in. She had decided for herself that there was no danger. She looked at the Mexican woman, who was scarcely more than a girl. Ellie's face warmed in recognition.

"María!"

The girl stared, and slowly she remembered Ellie. "*La Señora Donovan*. It has been so many years."

"Many years, Maria."

Before they had a chance to talk a young Mexican man rushed through the door, an ax in his hand as a weapon. He was looking for a fight until he saw Ellie and recognized her. He turned toward Webb and the other men, his eyes still hostile and demanding explanation. He held the ax where he could use it.

Without many details, Florentino explained the situation to him. He said they were looking for Clabe Donovan.

The young man, whose name was Pablo, shook his head.

"The Señor Donovan, he has not come here in many years. A while after the señora left, he left too, with all his men.

Later we heard he was killed in Texas. For years we heard nothing more. Maria and I, we married, and we needed a house. We thought no one would mind if we used this one."

Florentino said, "But Donovan is back."

Pablo nodded. "That is what we have heard, but he has not been to San Miguel. We hear he spends much of his time in Arroyo de Lopez. It is bigger, and a livelier place. *Cantinas*, gambling, women." He glanced regretfully at Ellie. "I am sorry, señora. I should not have said that."

Ellie's knowledge of Spanish was sketchy, but she understood that readily enough. She said, "He's changed. Like I told you, he never used to go there except when he had to. As for women . . ." Her lips drew tight. "Perhaps I should never have left him."

Webb said, "Strange he hasn't at least come back for a look at the place, if he loved it so much."

Ellie said, "Maybe he was bitter because I left him. Maybe this place has memories for him, like it has for me."

They stayed a while to rest. It didn't take long for the whole village to learn the Señora Donovan was back. It seemed the people all remembered her with affection. They came by twos and threes and half dozens to pay their respects, visit a while and go again. Ellie seemed to draw pleasure, now that she was here, in visiting with these old friends, recalling events so long forgotten or shoved aside in the dark corners of memory.

Pablo said, "We will move out of the house, señora. It is yours."

She shook her head. "No, keep it. I want you to have it. I would not have use for it, and I am pleased to know it is making a home for my friends."

Webb looked at his pocketwatch. He shook his head. "Gettin' late, Ellie. We better be on the move."

Florentino had stepped outdoors to look around. Now he rushed back, his face excited. "Mister Webb, something is happening down the creek. Looks like much excitement."

Stepping out the door, Webb saw a rising of dust, people running. A boy of eight or ten hurried toward the house, running as hard as he could.

"Los soldados!" he was shouting. *"Los soldados vienen!"* The soldiers are coming!

"Ellie," Webb shouted, "get out here quick! Run for the brush!"

The boy reached the house. Breathlessly he tried to tell what was happening in the village. Lieutenant Armendariz had ridden in with six men. He was looking for some *gringos*, three men and a women. The people had told him nothing, so he ripped the shirt off an old man's back and was lashing him now. Armendariz, the boy said, did not stop lashing people until they gave him what he wanted . . . or until they died. And this man was old. He would not last long.

Webb's first instinct was to get their horses and ride. They could be making tracks toward Arroyo de Lopez while Armendariz was delayed here. He made half a dozen steps in the direction of the horses before he halted, his shoulders slumped.

"We can't run," he said dejectedly. "This isn't these people's fight. It isn't fair to dump it in their laps. Ellie, you do like I told you: run for the brush. Don't let him find you."

"And us?" Florentino asked excitedly. "We will get this Armendariz, no?"

Webb said, "We'll do whatever we have to. Back away if we can, or fight if it comes to that. Let's get our horses."

In a moment they were spurring into a lope down the trail worn by decades of hoof traffic and cartwheels. They came around a pair of adobe houses and pulled up side by side.

An old man lay groveling in the dust, his shirt torn away, his back bleeding in streaks where the cruel lash had cut deep into naked flesh. Lieutenant Armendariz dropped the whip at sight of the three riders. They sat their horses in an even line some thirty feet from where Armendariz stood. In Webb's hand was the pistol, in Johnny's the rifle, in Florentino's the wicked shotgun. Armendariz stared in surprise. Then, slowly, a cruel grin crept across his dark face. He looked back over his shoulder where his six soldiers still sat on their poorly-fed horses. The men had held guns on the villagers who huddled fear-struck in front of the adobes. Now they swung the guns around to cover the Americans.

It was an impasse, a draw, for each side was ready to begin firing instantly. All that was needed was for someone to touch off the explosion.

The lieutenant spoke in Spanish, "Very effective, the whip. Usually it brings only information. This time it brings the *gringos*. If you will drop those guns, perhaps my men will not shoot you. Perhaps!"

Webb said, "We are as ready as they are. We can kill as many of you as you can kill of us."

The lieutenant's grin faded for only a moment, then came back, dry and mocking. "You are the same sheriff who tried to cross the river once before. Do you think I intend to let you get back again?"

"How did you find us so quickly?"

"This morning we stopped at a camp where an old man and a boy were fishing. We meant only to borrow a few fish. But we found horse tracks which led off a gravel bar. The old man did not wish to tell us anything at first. But the whip, it is good at persuasion."

Webb felt the rise of bitter anger. Florentino's jaw was set hard, his eyes a-glitter with hatred. He asked Webb, "Is this the man who killed Aparicio?"

Webb replied, "Yes."

Armendariz said, "Even with the guns in your hand, the advantage is mine. You are a man of conscience, *gringo*. Otherwise you would not have come to help one of so little value as this *viejo*, here in the dust. You can ride away from here if you choose. But if you do, I will take my vengeance on the people of this village. They have helped you."

He paused to watch the fury boil into Webb's face. "You do not like that, do you, *gringo*? You do not want these people on your conscience. That is why I have the advantage over you. I have no conscience. Believe me, I will do just what I say. I will come back, and the people here will answer for their help to you."

Florentino's voice was as quiet as the rattle of death. "No they won't. You are not leaving here!"

Armendariz saw the lethal intention in Florentino's eyes. Desperately he shouted at his men and reached for a pistol at his hips. He never touched it. Florentino's shotgun boomed. Armendariz reeled backward and sprawled in the dust of the street.

The soldiers' frightened horses began to rear and dance, and the men had their hands full. One soldier snapped a wild shot at Florentino but missed. The horse jumped, and the soldier landed on his shoulder, rolling in the dirt. He began clawing desperately for his dropped pistol. A villager grabbed it and jumped away. The soldier looked up in terror at the guns which faced him. *"No me mata!"* he shrilled. *Don't kill me!* "I am only a soldier. I do what I am told."

The other soldiers got their horses quieted down. Two of them had dropped their guns in the melee, and the others had lost their advantage. Seeing now that the fight was over almost without having begun, they let the guns drop from their fingers.

Webb asked them, "Any more guns?"

There were none.

"Go!" Webb ordered. "Never come back here. Understand? Never!"

"Never, *señor*," promised the one on the ground.

Webb knew they might not keep their word, but he doubted they could ever amount to much with Armendariz gone. Webb and his two men never relaxed their surveillance over the soldiers until the Mexicans turned their scrubby horses and headed out across the creek. Webb swung to the ground then. The villagers began to edge forward. Most of them formed a wide circle around the fallen Armendariz. A few began to pick up the weapons the soldiers had dropped.

Webb said, "Keep those guns. Hide them, because you may need them someday. If the soldiers come back, you can say the *gringos* took the guns."

Armendariz began to stir. He struggled for breath. Webb was surprised, for he had thought the blast had killed the lieutenant. But Florentino's aim had not been good. Only the outer edge of the shot pattern had struck Armendariz. That had been enough to knock the breath out of him and leave

a bloody wound in his side. One of the villagers picked up
Armendariz's gun to keep it out of the officer's reach.

Armendariz pushed himself into a sitting position, hands
clasped painfully over the wound where blood was seeping
out between his fingers. The people of San Miguel stared at
him in a smouldering hatred.

Florentino gritted, "I did a poor job. I will finish it." He
started to reload the shotgun. Webb reached out and pushed
the barrel down. "No, Florentino. It's one thing to shoot him
when he's standin' there reachin' for a gun. It's another thing
to shoot him after he's helpless."

One of the older villagers stepped up with his hat in his
hand. "Please, señor, we have suffered much from this man.
We would be forever in your debt if you would leave him
here."

Webb frowned.

The old man said, "*Señor*, we propose only to give him
justice."

Armendariz's face had been defiant. Now defiance began
to give way to fear. "*Gringo*, you must not do this. You are
an officer of the law, just as I am. You cannot leave me in
the hands of this rabble."

"What else could I do?"

"Take me with you."

Webb was sure that if they helped Armendariz the man
would turn on them at the first opportunity like a vicious
wolf released from a trap. "A few minutes ago you were
going to shoot us."

"Justice, *señor!* All I ask is justice!"

"Justice!" Webb's mouth twisted in a bitter smile. "I doubt
that you know what the word means. But I think you are
about to find out." He turned away. "Come on, Johnny, Florentino. Let's ride."

They got on their horses. One of the younger men of the
village reached up and pointed at Johnny's saddle. "*Señor,
por favor*, your rope."

Johnny considered a moment, glancing toward Webb, then
loosened the hornstring and dropped the rope into eager
brown hands.

Armendariz cried out, "For the love of God, don't leave me here!"

Johnny said, "Webb, you know what they're fixin' to do?"

Webb shrugged and kept himself from looking back. "It's none of our affair. He brought it on himself. We've got no responsibility to him."

They spurred their horses into a trot toward the adobe house where Ellie would be waiting. Surrounded by the vengeful villagers, Armendariz kept crying out to the Americans. His pleading turned into a shrill screaming as the men began to send the women and children away. The screaming went on even after the three riders had gone out of sight around a bend in the trail.

Webb's flesh crawled, but he didn't slow his horse, didn't even turn around in the saddle to look.

12

THEY PUT SAN MIGUEL BEHIND THEM A LITTLE WHILE BE-
fore dark, and Webb was glad to go. He didn't know
precisely what the villagers had done to Armendariz, nor did
he care to find out. The thought of it sent a chill down his
back. Later on, if questions were ever asked, the villagers
would say the officer had been killed by three unknown riders from *el otro lado*, the other side. Armendariz's own soldiers would back them in that. Perhaps the next officer sent
to the river country would protect the people instead of preying on them.

Because Ellie asked him to, the young man Pablo caught
up his own horse, one of the small-bodied, long-tailed Mexican kind, and went along to show the easiest way to Arroyo
de Lopez. Webb wanted to be well away from San Miguel
before night. He thought it unlikely that any of Armendariz's
soldiers would come back, but just in case . . .

After riding in darkness a couple of hours, they stopped
to rest. At daylight they arose and moved again, taking their
time. It was only a short distance to the village they sought,
and Webb had no intention of riding into it in broad daylight
anyway, not without first keeping it under surveillance a long
time.

They came upon a sluggish creek, where wild longhorn
cattle broke into a run at the sight of them. Pablo said, "My

friends, we are close now. Up this creek half an hour's ride
is Arroyo de Lopez."

Webb asked, "Are you leaving us, Pablo?"

The young Mexican looked back at Ellie, who rode in the
rear. "I have no quarrel with the *Señor* Donovan. But, if the
señora wants me to stay, I will stay.

Often during the ride he had looked back over his shoulder, his troubled gaze studying the young woman. Loyalty
to family was deeply ingrained in the Mexican people. It was
hard for Pablo to comprehend how a woman could help in
the tracking down of her own husband. She might kill him
herself, perhaps, in a sudden flare of jealousy, but never help
someone else to do it. In his limited experience Pablo had
never seen the like of this.

"Donovan is no longer the same as when she married
him," Webb said, trying to explain. "He has done much
wrong, hurt many people."

"Has he hurt the *señora?*"

Webb pondered. "Yes, and no." Truly, Clabe Donovan had
not done any direct wrong to Ellie herself, unless it was to
have led her into a fugitive's life in the beginning. Webb
said, "Pablo, if you had a faithful old dog, but he went mad
and became a danger to other people, you would be obliged
to kill him no matter how much you loved him."

Pablo observed, "A man, *señor*, is not a mad dog."

"He can be, sometimes. I think this one is."

Pablo turned back and pulled his horse in beside Ellie's.
He asked her if she wanted him to stay. She replied, "Pablo,
these are good men here. They may need help."

Pablo nodded. "Then I will stay."

They approached the village with caution. Although he
could not see the whole place, Webb could tell it was much
bigger than San Miguel. Pablo's eyes swelled, for to him this
was a metropolis. It lay on a large north-south road, one that
evidently carried a fair amount of commerce. They pulled
off into the brush to avoid meeting a peddler who approached
from the south in a hardware-laden two-wheel cart, drawn
by a sharp-hipped mule. Webb could hear a multitude of
mongrel dogs rushing to challenge the peddler. The man's

whip cracked as one of the dogs moved too close to the gray mule. The dog yowled. A boy's voice cried sharp insults, but the peddler paid no mind.

From somewhere out of sight came the ring of a blacksmith's hammer, the ee-aww of a burro. Webb did not see much activity. But then, Mexican villages seldom had the constant shifting movement, the street-crowding foot and horse traffic that so often was found in towns on the north side of the river. Life was slower here, and the demands on it were less.

"Pablo," Webb asked, "do you have any idea where Donovan stays?"

Pablo shook his head. "I have been to this place only once before in my life. I was but a boy then, and I came with my father."

Webb had forgotten how little the average Mexican traveled. A trip to another valley a few miles away might be the longest a man took in a lifetime if he was a farmer and had no particular reason to travel. Indeed, some looked upon people of other villages as foreigners. The state capitol was as far away for many of them as Europe might seem to an American, and Mexico City had as well be on the moon. This isolation manifested itself even in speech. Each town or village developed a slightly different dialect from that of its neighbors, with phrases and colloquialisms which indelibly marked a man's origin.

Webb leaned against his horse and stared across the saddle at that part of the village he could see through the green foliage of the mesquite. "No tellin' how many men might be with him in there," he said to Johnny and Florentino. "We'd be foolish to go a-ridin' in there in the daylight, not even knowin' where to start lookin' at. We'll just pull off aways and wait out the rest of the day. Come dark, we'll have to go in and try to nose him out."

Florentino dropped back beside Pablo. They talked a while in a fast-clipped Spanish that lost Webb somewhere along the line. At length Florentino announced in English, "Mister Webb, Pablo and I, we have decided. We two, we go down into the town when night comes. We are both Mexican. Who will notice us? We look, we ask questions. Maybe we find out where Donovan is."

Webb said, "Remember, Florentino, Donovan knows you. If he sees you . . ."

"It is many years ago. I have changed. But I will stay away from him if I can."

Although Webb didn't like the idea, he knew it made sense. And he had no ideas of his own. "All right, but promise me you'll be careful. Remember, you have a new son. You have to think of him and of Consuela."

"I will remember them. But I also remember Aparicio, and Mister Joe."

This was rough hill country. Webb chose for their waiting place a hill which overlooked the town from the south. It had a fair covering of scrub brush and cactus. Webb decided to tie the horses on the off side and spend the day watching from the hilltop. Moving the long way around the hill, they pulled far off on a tangent, once to avoid meeting a couple of young boys who were picking up dry firewood and dropping it into a pair of large, dried-out, willow-switch baskets tied across the back of a gotch-eared, sleepy-eyed old burro. On the off side of the hill, where they left the horses, Ellie sat down in the thin shade of a mesquite. She hadn't said much this morning. She seemed to want to be left alone.

Johnny Willet built a small fire and put the coffee pot on to heat. He and Florentino and Pablo had staked the horses, loosening the cinches but not taking the saddles off. A stroke of bad luck might force the five to leave here in a hurry, and it might not give them time to resaddle.

Climbing the hill afoot, Webb disturbed a small string of multi-colored Spanish goats which were browsing around on the scattering of low brush.

Webb picked a shady spot which gave him a view over most of the town. The goats settled down to eating again, although the strong-smelling old billy kept eyeing Webb with suspicion. Webb was glad for the company. He figured if he was seen from down in town, he probably would be mistaken for one of the goats. No one would pay him any attention. Through his spyglass he watched the two boys enter town

with their burro and their load of firewood, the baskets bobbing up and down gently with the slow, lazy movement of
the animal.

After a while *siesta* time came. Little movement remained
on the street, and that little was therefore hard to miss. At
each sign of movement Webb would swing the glass around
for a look, hoping to catch sight of someone who was ob-
viously *gringo*, someone who didn't belong. But if such *gringos* were here, they had adopted the Mexican custom of
siesta. They weren't stirring about.

Johnny brought Webb a cup of coffee, some cold bread
and bacon. "Man's got to eat, Webb, whether he wants to or
not. See anything?"

"Nothin' that'll help us any."

"Maybe they're not here. Maybe they went across the river
on another raid."

Webb's face furrowed. "We'll sit here and wait if it takes
a week!"

Through the long afternoon the still summer heat pushed
down oppressively. Webb fought flies and the heat and the
helpless impatience. Miserable as he felt, he knew how much
more miserable the wait must be for Ellie. She remained
below, asking no sympathy but keeping her own counsel and
suffering alone.

Late in the afternoon a welcome breeze stirred from the
south. It was not cool, but it served to carry away the flies
and lift some of the still, intolerable heat. Down in town,
people began stirring again. Women and girls carried vessels
down to the creek to fetch water. Children played, an occasional vagrant scrap of their shouting and laughter reaching
Webb on the hillside. Men appeared in the fields to do some
hoeing amid the corn. Webb would watch through the spyglass until he had to put the instrument down and rest his
eyes.

Discouragement settled over him, for all the people he saw
appeared to be Mexican.

Suddenly he straightened, bringing up the glass and fo-
cusing. He saw two men on horseback. The horses were bigger and fatter than those which belonged to the people here.

They were Texas horses, no mistake about that. And the men were *gringos*, Webb knew even at that distance. It showed in the clothes they wore, the cowboy-style hats on their heads. It was apparent in the heedless way they rode down the street, forcing even the women to move aside.

"Johnny," Webb spoke with a tone of excitement, "come look."

Johnny took the glass. A grim smile slowly came over his face. "I think we finally struck gold."

At nightfall Florentino and Pablo began tightening their cinches for the ride down into town. Webb laid his hand on the neck of the horse Florentino had been riding. He looked worriedly into the face of the Mexican who had so long been his friend. "Don't be takin' risks, Florentino. Don't hang around where the *gringos* are. Somebody might recognize you. And don't stay a minute longer than you have to."

He started to turn away, then stopped. "Florentino, if you see any sign of my brother . . ."

He broke off. It seemed disloyal even to entertain the thought that Sandy could be here. Yet the fear had tormented him ever since the day he had ridden back from his fruitless mission to find the Dry Fork bank robbed.

Webb hadn't finished what he was going to say. Florentino spoke, "If I see him, what?"

"If you see him, tell me. Don't keep it a secret."

Florentino said gravely, "If I see him, I won't lie to you."

The two rode away. Webb walked back to the camp where the cookfire was only hot coals. He poured himself a cup of coffee and glanced at the silent woman who sat with her knees gathered up under her, her face hidden in her arms. Webb's mouth twisted. Then he sat to sip the coffee and wait. Just wait, and wait . . .

It seemed hours before he heard the strike of hoofs. He sat stiffly, pistol in his hand. He heard Florentino's quiet voice: "Mister Webb."

"Up here, Florentino."

The two riders came on and dismounted. In the moonlight Webb could see victory in Florentino's face.

"He is here, Mister Webb. Donovan is here."

A flare of triumph came to Webb. It subsided, and he looked around for Ellie. She still sat where she had been all afternoon.

"Where's he at, Florentino?"

"Right now he is in the *cantina*. But we do not want to try for him there. Too many of his men are with him. Six, seven men, I think, some *gringos*, a couple of Mexican *pistoleros*. *Ladrones*, all of them. Bad men."

Webb looked down, clenching his fist. "And Sandy?"

Florentino shook his head. "No, Mister Webb, and I do not lie to you. He is not in the *cantina*."

Webb's shoulders straightened a little. Maybe Sandy wasn't here at all. Maybe he never had been. Maybe the whole idea had been a mistake from the start.

He asked, "If we don't take Donovan in the *cantina*, where do we get a chance at him?"

"Pablo and me, we went among the people of the village. We ask many questions . . . not big questions, just little ones. Donovan, he has a house. He lives there alone." He looked around, evidently searching for Ellie and seeming glad she wasn't near enough to hear. "Almost alone. A girl of the village, she lives with him. She is in the *cantina* with him now."

"Did you see Donovan himself?"

Florentino nodded excitedly. "I look through the window. His back is turn to me, but I see him. I know that back, for I have seen it many times. And the black sombrero, it was on the floor at his feet."

"You found out where his house is?"

Florentino glanced at Pablo and nodded. "*Si*. We find it."

A little coffee was left in Webb's cup, but suddenly it seemed cold and bitter. He flung it out upon the ground. A chill passed through him. "We'll go there, and we'll wait for him to come to us."

He turned to Johnny, who had come in time to hear most

of the conversation. "Johnny, will you go tell Ellie?" Then, thinking again, he said, "No, don't. I'll tell her."

Dogs picked them up as they rode down into Arroyo de Lopez, but no one paid attention because the dogs would bark at anything that moved. The riders themselves were as silent as the black shadows of night that they rode in. They kept away from the small open windows of the adobes, and the timid patches of dim candlelight that cautiously peeped out. To get rid of weight and to free the packhorse for Donovan, they untied the pack and left it near the door of a poor little brush-roofed adobe which looked as if its occupants could use the food. Moving away, Johnny brushed against a dry, tight fence made picket-style of the wicked, spike-edged stems of the *ocatillo* cactus. It was a lightweight fence, but its thorns would turn back a bull. Johnny squalled out in pain. He clapped his hand over his mouth after the damage already was done. They watched and listened nervously, expecting trouble. But nobody seemed to have heard. Nobody came.

They left the horses in a pool of blackness a hundred feet from Donovan's house. Ellie would stay with the horses, and Pablo was to stay beside Ellie. Webb had suggested the Mexican start home before any trouble began, but Pablo decided the good *señora* might need help. He owed her that in return for the house in San Miguel.

Nervousness coiled like a steel spring in Webb Matlock as he walked toward the Donovan adobe, his hand slick with cold sweat against the gunbutt. The house was still and dark. Webb and Johnny and Florentino leaned against the dry, crumbly wall, listening, holding their breath.

"Florentino," Webb whispered, "you stay out here in the shadows and watch. Don't show yourself unless somethin' goes wrong. Johnny and me, we'll try and take him after he goes in the house."

Florentino nodded. *"Buena suerte."* Good luck.

The front door was open. Theft was rare among the people who lived in these villages because everyone knew everyone else. A thief could not go long undiscovered, or unpunished. This was poor country for a locksmith.

Inside, Webb and Johnny stood a while and studied the dark room until they could pick out the few pieces of furniture: chairs, table, bed. There was not even a stove. Cooking would be done outdoors in a round, earthen oven. A strong smell of spilled liquor clung to the place, liquor that had soaked into the dirt floor in considerable amount. Webb could imagine the raucous drinking bouts that must have been thrown inside these barren walls.

He could also detect the faint lingering of cheap perfume, and he was glad Ellie had remained outside.

Johnny asked, "Webb, do you reckon Ellie can take it when she sees Clabe comin'?"

"Why not?"

"She's acted kind of strange today. Like she was with us but still alone, if you know what I mean."

Webb nodded solemnly. "In her place, would you do different?"

"I don't know; that's what bothers me. Was I her and I saw Clabe fixin' to walk into a trap, it'd be all I could do to keep from hollerin' to him, tellin' him to run like the devil was after him. How do you know she won't?"

"She's come this far. I don't think she'll break down now."

"I hope not. I just wish I could be as sure."

Webb took a chair in one corner, facing the open door. Johnny sat on a bench in the corner opposite the front of the room. They sat in silence, listening. From outside they could hear the quiet life of the village passing the early hours of the night—dogs barking at the edge of town, a cow bawling for a calf, a woman calling her children to bed. Someone strummed a melancholy tune on a guitar, and a voice lifted gently in a melancholy song of love and death.

Webb looked out at one strange noise and saw a lank-bodied, long-nosed old sow walking down the street, her small brood following right along, trying for milk every time she paused a moment.

After a long time he heard someone walking slowly up

the dusty street toward the house, feet dragging a little. Webb's heartbeat quickened. He pushed to his feet, the gun ready. In the darkness he could see the dim outline of Johnny Willet, who had done the same.

They waited, their tenseness building as the footsteps drew nearer and nearer the door. Finally Webb thought sure he was about to see the figure of Clabe Donovan framed in the doorway, dark against the starlight. But the man—whoever he was—passed on by the house and kept walking. He began to sing softly to himself in a voice that carried no melody. It was a Mexican song, a Mexican voice. Not Clabe Donovan.

Webb let his breath out slowly and wiped the palms of his hands against his shirt. He sat again in the creaky chair, wishing the tenseness would leave him.

He had the feeling it wouldn't be much longer now. Donovan would be here directly. Clabe Donovan, dead these many years and now back to life again. A different man now than he had been before, a savage, vengeful man no longer possessed of those few good qualities which once had made even his enemies respect him. Enemies like his one-time friend, Webb Matlock.

Webb heard the footsteps. Steeling himself, he pushed up from the chair. He could hear a man's voice speaking softly. The words were Spanish, but even Webb's untrained ear could tell that the Spanish was slurred by a careless *gringo* accent. A woman giggled foolishly.

The pair appeared in the doorway, their silhouettes plain. They were a tall man with a big sombrero and a slender woman whose full skirt almost swept the floor. The man embraced her, then began feeling beside the door for a table he knew was there. He found the table and set down a bottle that went clunk as it fell over. He righted it quickly, both he and the woman laughing. His back to Webb and Johnny, the man fished in his pocket and came up with a match. He struck it on his bootsole and lighted a single thick wax candle that stood in a saucer on the table.

Webb's voice was so steady that it surprised him.

"Hands up! Don't make a move, Clabe Donovan!"

The man stiffened, his hands flat on the table. For the space of several seconds he stood like that, his back still turned. Slowed by drink, he was plainly too stunned to know what to do.

The girl turned and saw the guns. She shrieked, her eyes going wide as silver *pesos*, her hands lifting to cover her mouth.

Webb said, "Turn around slow, Clabe. Make a single suspicious move and I'll shoot to kill."

Donovan still seemed stunned. "Who is it?"

"Webb Matlock. I've come to take you back across the river."

"You got no authority here."

"I got all the authority I need, right here in my hand. Turn around now, Clabe. Turn slow and careful."

Some sardonic humor seemed to move in Donovan. He began to laugh. Then, slowly and deliberately, he turned.

Webb's mouth dropped open, and he cast a surprised glance at Johnny Willet. The resemblance was uncanny, but this was not Clabe Donovan.

This was Clabe's brother, Morg!

13

"WHAT'S THE MATTER, WEBB MATLOCK?" MORG DONO-
van laughed contemptuously. "Somethin' give you a
shock?"

For a moment Webb was speechless. "Where's Clabe at,
Morg?"

"Where he's been all these years. In that graveyard over
at Dry Fork."

"But we thought . . ." Webb trailed off. "Then we were
right, all that time. It *was* Clabe who died that night, breakin'
out of jail."

Morg nodded. "Blown to pieces by a shotgun in the hands
of an old fool who couldn't have wiped the dust off Clabe's
boots." The sardonic humor was gone from Morg Donovan
now. A somber chill crept into his eyes. "I swore I'd get
even for what happened to my brother. I've made a start."

"But you're through now, Morg. We're takin' you back
across the river, and there's no Clabe Donovan to get you
free this time."

Donovan said scornfully, "You know how far it is to the
river? You'll never get there with me. You may not even
leave Arroyo de Lopez. What if I decide just to sit down
here and call your bluff? You're not the kind of man who
would shoot me in cold blood."

"Wrong, Morg." Webb's voice was bitter. "Balk on me

and I *will* kill you, right where you're at. I remember the way you blasted down Uncle Joe Vickers at the wagon-yard in Dry Fork. You didn't give him a chance."

"He's the old devil who killed Clabe. I owed him that shootin'."

"Slow and easy now, Morg, unbuckle your gunbelt and drop it."

All this time the good-looking young Mexican woman had stood frozen, not comprehending the words but grimly certain of their import.

Ellie Donovan was unable to stand the suspense any longer. At this moment she stepped in the door, her face tense. "Clabe?" Morg Donovan turned. She gasped in surprise at the sudden realization that this was not her husband.

Morg—with the quick wit that had always been his brother's—took advantage of the distraction. In one motion he ripped off his sombrero, whirled and snuffed out the candle with a sweep of the big hat. In the darkness he roughly shoved both women aside and leaped for the open door. Webb stood helpless, afraid to fire because of the women.

From outside he heard a sharp thud and a grunt and a body sliding on the bare ground. Webb sprinted across the small room and out the door.

Florentino Rodriguez said, "Is all right, Mister Webb. I hit him over the head as he is come out." He held the shotgun up for inspection against the stars. "I hope the barrel, she is not bent."

The stunned Morg Donovan swayed on hands and knees, shaking his head and groaning.

The Mexican woman came out of shock. She took a horrified look at Morg Donovan, then turned and ran screaming down the street.

Florentino bent and grabbed hold of Morg Donovan's arm. "Mister Webb, this place is pretty quick a hornet's nest."

Webb grabbed Morg's other arm and helped the outlaw to his feet. Donovan's knees were wobbly. Webb turned toward the dark place where the horses were. "Let's haul our freight."

Ellie ran beside them, still looking at Morg. "But, Webb, this isn't Clabe," she protested in confusion.

Webb wished he had time to explain. For that matter, he wished he fully understood it himself. "It never was, Ellie. Clabe is dead."

He thought Ellie was going to fall. She stumbled, caught herself and stood a moment with her hands over her face. Then, recovering, she hurried to catch up with the men.

Morg was still groggy as they reached the horses. Quickly Webb tied the man's hands with a strip of rawhide he had brought for the purpose. He tied one end of the rawhide through the fork of the saddle so Morg could not get loose. From down the street came the rising sounds of a village awakened, the barking of dogs, the cries of frightened women, the wild shouts of excited men.

Two men came running hard around the corner of Donovan's adobe house. They heard rather than saw the movement of Webb's group in the shadows. One of the men leveled a pistol. The other knocked the gun upward just as it fired.

"You fool!" Webb heard him cry, "you might hit Donovan!"

Webb took a firm grip on Donovan's bridle reins. "Spur 'em!"

The horses clattered out across the bare, packed ground into the moonlight. A chorus went up. Someone fired, but the shooting stopped as abruptly as it started.

Carrying Donovan, the packhorse lagged. Webb's arm was stretched backward to the point that it was painful to hold onto the reins. He pulled his own mount down to get slack, then took a wrap around the horn and touched spurs to his horse. The impact caught the led animal in midstride and almost jerked him to his knees. The groggy Donovan grunted. After that, there was no more difficulty. Donovan's horse stayed up.

The creek lay ahead, its waters murmuring peacefully in the night. Webb and his group spurred into it, shattering its quiet, raising a silver spray in the moonlight. The cool splash of water was refreshing to Webb. In half a dozen long strides his horse gained the far bank. Webb reined up a moment to look back. He could hear horses, the hectic clatter of pursuit.

"The brush yonder," he said, pointing. "We can't outrun them. Maybe we can shake loose from them in the thicket."

Water hitting his face had helped bring Donovan back to full consciousness. With his hands tied he had a strong grip on the saddlehorn. To fall out of the saddle while tied to it could mean dragging, and many a man had died dragging from a horse, his ribs caved in by a hoof or his head broken against a tree.

"Matlock," he complained, "you're a-fixin' to get me drug to death."

Webb said coldly, "Just stay in the saddle. That part is up to you." He didn't slow down.

Ahead, a heavy stand of mesquite brush and catclaw choked a wide draw that angled back toward the creek. Webb rode into it full tilt, the others right with him. They ducked their heads against the lash of thorny mesquite that scratched at their faces and ripped at their clothes. Morg Donovan cursed because he could not raise his arms for protection as the others could. He could only duck his head and hope he did not lose his big sombrero. Webb did not sympathize with him.

They rode deep into the brush before they stopped to listen. They could hear horses behind them.

"Gettin' closer," Webb whispered. "Don't anybody make a sound."

The pursuers fanned out and entered the thicket. Listening, Webb tried to tell how many there were. It was hard to gauge, maybe six, eight, even a dozen. The outlaws had slowed to a walk, and they pushed with caution through the hostile tangle. Webb bent low in the saddle, trying not to present a silhouette. It was so quiet here he almost fancied he could hear his watch ticking. He could hear the constrained breath of Ellie and Johnny and the two Mexicans above the whisper of brush, the soft padding of hoofs, the squeaking of saddle leather. For a time the pursuit drew inexorably nearer. Then the riders began veering away.

Donovan had sat with a confident air about him, waiting

for his men to come. Now it seemed they were going to miss him. He shouted, "Over here, boys! It's me!"

Webb pounced on him, clapping his hands over Donovan's mouth and almost pulling the outlaw from the saddle. Donovan made a desperate grab at the horn to keep from falling. Webb kept his hands over the man's mouth a moment and listened. Once more the riders were heading in their direction.

One of the men shouted, "Where you at, Morg?"

"Just holler again," called another. "We'll find you."

Webb pressed the cold muzzle of his pistol against the back of Morg Donovan's head. He muttered, "Make another sound and I'll blow your damned head off!"

Donovan's eyes rolled. He held his silence.

The riders kept working through the brush, but they missed their mark. They moved on by, the nearest passing twenty yards away. Webb held the muzzle tight against Donovan's neck. The man kept quiet.

Finally the riders were gone, although the sound of their search still continued.

"All right, Morg," Webb gritted, "I didn't aim to do this, but now I will." He pulled a handkerchief from his pocket. "Open your mouth."

"That thing's dirty," Donovan protested.

"Your fault, not mine. Open up."

Donovan opened his mouth, and Webb wadded the handkerchief into it. He pulled another handkerchief from Donovan's own hip pocket. He ran this one across Donovan's mouth and tied the ends behind the man's neck.

They could still hear the riders working through the brush. Ellie Donovan had pulled up beside Webb as if drawing strength from him. He reached out and touched her hand.

Finally he heard someone far off say, "This is damn foolishness. They could be in this thicket anyplace, waitin' to blast our heads off without us even seein' them."

Webb couldn't make out the reply, but he surmised that it was in agreement. The riders pulled back, leaving the thicket. They congregated on open ground at the edge of the draw. Webb could hear the sharp-edged rise of voices tangled in dispute. He couldn't understand much of it, but he heard a man say finally, "It's a long way to the Rio Grande."

After that the men pulled away. Webb held still until all sound of pursuit was gone. He sagged, some of the wound-up tension slowly loosening—temporarily, at least.

Webb looked at his companions' faces and could feel the anxiety that remained there. "All right," he spoke, "we better be on the move. That *pistolero* was right. It's a long way to the Rio Grande."

Pablo had done his work and more than Webb had ever expected. He sent the young man home to San Miguel with his gratitude.

Riding out then, Webb took his bearings on the north star. Terrain might vary, and a man might ride into a strange land where he had no landmarks to guide his way. But, when all else failed him, there still were the stars, constant and unchanging. In point of miles, the shortest way to the Rio would be to follow the north star. They might come across obstacles that would hold them up, that would force them to detour. But, as long as he could see the north star, they would never really be lost.

They moved carefully out of the brush, taking their time. They knew Donovan's men might be waiting somewhere, listening. In the clear, they paused a bit to listen too. They caught no sound of anyone hunting them, but Webb would bet that someone was. They rode a couple of miles before Webb saw fit to stop and take the gag from Donovan's mouth. "Next time you try another stunt like you pulled a while ago, that gag goes back in," he said roughly.

Donovan was relieved to be rid of the thing. He drew up saliva and spat, cleaning his mouth of the dry and dusty taste. "You're a fool, Matlock. You think them boys of mine went back to town to forget things over a bottle of *tequila?* You think they don't have a good notion where you're headed with me?"

Webb said evenly, "The point is, *we've* got you, they haven't."

"You'll never get me to the river. Ain't no way you can make it before daylight. Come sunup, when the boys can see, they'll close in on you like hounds on a rabbit."

"We're not rabbits, Morg."

"You'll wish you was. You'll wish you could just run down a hole and pull it in after you."

Webb succumbed a while to a burning compulsion to run the horses, to put some quick distance between themselves and Arroyo de Lopez. But he knew the mounts couldn't stand the pace long, not and have reserve strength left. He pulled the horses down to a trot.

Morg Donovan snorted. "Make you feel better to run, Matlock? Run all you want to. You still got to cross that river, and you'll never do it."

Webb's eyes narrowed. His voice was sharp as flint. "You're not gettin' away, Morg, just get that through your skull. Whatever happens to me, I'll have one bullet left for you. And I'll use it!"

For a minute their eyes met, stabbing, and hatred leaped between them hot and keen.

They moved in a steady trot through the darkness, cutting across the rough and rocky rangeland, through the brush, over the cactus-strewn Mexican prairies, across the dry creeks and washes. They were wasting miles, seeking their way through. Webb wished they could strike a good trail leading northward, but he knew it would be risky. Donovan's men would be using the roads and trails, trying to beat them to the river.

Webb stayed in the lead, Donovan's horse trailing half a length behind at the end of the reins. Ellie rode beside Webb, on the opposite side from Morg Donovan. Johnny and Florentino brought up the rear, looking behind them for pursuit.

Ellie kept turning her head, glancing at Morg. Amazing how much Morg resembled Clabe Donovan now. Webb could remember that there had always been a likeness, but Morg had been somewhat the younger in those times so long past, and the resemblance was not so pronounced as it had become now. Same size, same build, same general features. Only when you looked him full in the face could you readily tell the difference. In this moonlight, with the dark shadow cast by the black sombrero, it was hard to get a look at his face.

After a long time Ellie asked, "Morg, why the masquerade? Why did you want everybody to think you were Clabe?"

Morg Donovan stared at Ellie, his eyes detesting her. "Because Clabe Donovan was somebody! He was a real man, Clabe was. You never appreciated him."

Evenly she said, "I loved him, Morg, you know that."

"Loved him? Then how come you ran off and left him?"

"I couldn't stand the life we were leading. I begged him to quit. He promised he would, but he didn't do it. Just one more time, he always said, just one more time and he would call it quits. But I knew he wouldn't quit until they killed him. I couldn't stand it anymore."

Morg said with an ancient bitterness, "And finally they did kill him, killed him because he was caught tryin' to get me out of trouble. But I swore that wouldn't be the end of it. I swore I'd pay back everybody who had a hand in what happened to Clabe."

Webb asked, "How come it took so many years to start?"

"We needed money, me and the few that was left. We went down into Mexico and tried to rob a mint. It was a crazy thing to try. I got wounded and caught. One of the other boys was caught with me, and a couple got killed. I spent years in a prison down yonder, a Mexican prison. You know what they can be like, Matlock. The boy that was with me, he died, and dyin' was the easy way out. But I lived because I couldn't afford to die. I still had debts to pay."

Now that Morg had begun, he seemed compelled to tell all of it. His voice was as grim as blood. "I done a lot of thinkin' while I was in prison. I knew how Clabe had died. It came to me that with his face all blasted away, nobody could really swear it was Clabe. Could've been me, for all anybody could prove. Now, Morg Donovan never meant much to anybody, except to Clabe. But Clabe Donovan, he was really somebody, a legend. Shame for him to die the way he did.

"It came to me that maybe he didn't have to be dead after all. He could still be alive, through me. After all, I never had amounted to no hell of a lot. All I had to do was pretend I was Clabe, and Clabe would be alive, all over again. If he'd lasted longer, Clabe Donovan would've been a man they'd write books about, like Jesse James and them. Man like that, he don't ever really die because folks don't ever forget him. I figured I owed that to Clabe. I could be him. I could bring him back to life and make him known the way he ought to've been."

He fell silent, remembering. Webb said, "One thing you overlooked, Morg, you never were the man Clabe was. You didn't have his brain for makin' plans, for gettin' things done."

"I was younger, wilder. I left a lot of that behind me in prison. Time I broke out of there, I was a lot smarter than when I went in. I figured I could use Clabe's name and do proud by it. Prison gave me lots of time to plan. It didn't take me long to round up a couple or three of the old hands and to find some new ones as good as the others had been. Far as the new hands knew, I really was Clabe Donovan. The old ones, they kept their mouths shut. I lined things up with Bronc Tomlin. We started with horses and cattle first because they was easy, and we needed money. From that, I figured we'd work on up to banks, and even trains. Wouldn't be long till Clabe Donovan would be known from New York City to the Pacific Ocean."

Webb said, "You couldn't go on forever, wearin' a dead man's boots."

Morg replied, "A year or two, then I figured I would just fade away. They would always wonder what had happened to Clabe. Makes it even better, don't it, when folks don't really know? They worry over it, and they don't ever forget. They talk about it as long as they live. They'd never forget Clabe Donovan, not in a hundred years."

Webb said, "When we take you back, everybody is goin' to know the truth. They'll know Clabe Donovan is dead."

Morg shook his head. "Who's to tell? Not a one of you is ever goin' back across that river!"

Webb glanced at Ellie, and then back to Morg. "Would you kill a woman?"

Morg said bitterly, "I'd kill *her*. Think I didn't hear about her, gettin' herself involved with the Twin Forks sheriff, the very one who put her husband in jail, the man responsible for gettin' Clabe killed? Her, the only woman Clabe ever looked at twice? The night I shot the old man who killed Clabe, I came within an inch of killin' her too. I stood and looked at her through the window and started to shoot. Then I thought, better to kill the sheriff she intended on marryin'. Make her a widow twice over. Let her live to worry over that and wonder why."

Webb saw that Ellie was crying softly. He remembered the night of which Morg spoke. He remembered how shaken Ellie had been because she had thought she saw Clabe Donovan standing in the darkness. He shuddered now, realizing how close she had come to dying that night.

He said, "Morg, you've let hatred twist your mind until you're crazy. Any man who could even think of shootin' down a helpless woman . . ."

"She belonged to Clabe!"

"But Clabe was dead."

Morg shook his head violently. "No, he wasn't dead. I wasn't goin' to let him stay dead. I was bringin' him back to life, and she belonged to him." He looked wildly at Ellie, his eyes accusing her. "She belonged to him, I tell you. She belonged to Clabe!"

Webb's mouth went dry. Great God, the man *was* crazy! He had almost come to believe he *was* Clabe Donovan.

Webb licked dry lips and tore his gaze from Morg Donovan. "Come on, let's push. We want to get as close to that river as we can before daylight."

They rode as hard as Webb thought they dared, consistent with saving the horses. He followed the north star and found his way blocked periodically by washouts that they had to circle around, by a creek too deep to try until they hunted and found a natural ford. All this, he realized in a helpless churn of anxiety, was costing them time.

Eventually they came to a road that seemed to head gen-

erally northward. They halted at the edge of it. Webb took
out his pocketwatch and tilted it so the moon fell full on the
dial. "A little past three in the mornin'," he said. Wouldn't
be much sign of light for a couple of hours yet.

"How far would you say it is to the river, Morg?"

Morg Donovan threw back his head contemptuously.
"Think I'd tell you? Find out for your ownself." He paused,
drawing some pleasure from the fact that he was able to
withhold knowledge that Webb needed. "I'll tell you this:
it's too far to make it before daylight. And come daylight,
you won't make it anyhow."

Frustrated by the delays they had encountered in trying to
cut across country, Webb was tempted to use the road
awhile. Surely the road would seek the easiest way north and
save them time. But there was a danger . . .

Florentino said urgently, "Mister Webb, I think I hear
something. Listen!"

Webb listened but heard nothing. Florentino's ears must
be better than his, he thought, or the Mexican was letting
imagination get the better of him. Then the sound came to
Webb too.

Hoofbeats, coming up the road.

Webb waved his hand. "Back!" They pulled away from
the road, and he was glad they hadn't crossed it, for their
tracks might show in the moonlight. The road hadn't been
used much. They stepped to the ground.

"Open your mouth, Morg," he said. "The gag."

"Not again!" Morg protested.

"I don't trust you. Open up."

When he had gagged the outlaw, he caught his horse's
nose and that of Donovan's mount to keep the animals from
nickering. In the night the sound of the approaching riders
grew stronger. Presently the men came by, pushing their
horses along in an easy lope. Seven riders.

When they had passed, Johnny Willet asked in a nervous
voice, "Reckon them was Donovan's men?"

Webb nodded. "I doubt anybody else would have business
travelin' this road at such an hour. They were his, all right."

He took the gag from Morg's mouth. Morg spat, face

twisting at the dry taste which lingered. Gruffly he said, "Sure, they was my boys. Got any doubt now what'll happen when you start across that river? You got no chance, Matlock, no chance atall."

A prickling sensation explored up and down Webb's backside. His mouth went flat and grim. "Well," he said, "the road's out. We got to keep movin' cross-country. Let's get at it."

He could see the weariness bearing down on Ellie Donovan's thin shoulders. She spoke not a word in complaint but rode in sad-faced silence, her mind probably numbed. Sympathy for her was like an ache in Webb, but he knew nothing to say that would alleviate her misery. He held silent and hoped she knew how he felt.

The eastern sky began to pale, and daylight crept cautiously over this unfamiliar desert land. Webb glanced often toward the deepening red tinge that arose in the east. Usually he welcomed the dawn, but this time he wished he could hold it back. He wasn't ready and wouldn't be ready until they had swum that river and could put Mexico behind them.

Sunrise. Warm light bathed the cactus-dotted prairie and the irregular pattern of the brushlands. Webb sat nervously in the saddle, his gaze constantly working the land before him, studying every object that aroused suspicion, always finding it to be a tree or a bush, or perhaps a wandering burro. The torturing question kept burning in his brain: how far to the river?

A gunshot sent his heart leaping in alarm. He bent low in the saddle, instinctively drawing his pistol. Wide-eyed, he looked around him. He saw dismay in Ellie Donovan's eyes, triumph in Morg's. Two more shots followed.

"Signal," Webb said. "Somebody's spotted us, and he's signaled for the others."

Johnny Willet swallowed, looking for signs of whoever had found them. He saw nothing. With the echoes that rocketed through the cool morning air, it was hard to tell even where the shots had come from.

"We must not be far from the river," Webb guessed. "They fanned out to watch for us." He figured the Donovan bunch would have spread out back from the river far enough that they would be able to gather again before their quarry reached the line.

He saw that Ellie was scared. "Ellie, you feel up to a hard ride?"

She nodded. He said, "All right, then, let's run for it."

He spurred into a lope. The others followed him. The horse's hoofs drummed hard, churning dust from a thin turf of sparse grass. The brush seemed to fly by. They came to a thicket, but Webb never slowed. He ducked his head and threw up his arms for protection and spurred on through. The switchy green mesquite limbs bent and clawed and then whipped back into place. He lost part of his shirt but never looked back.

He heard Florentino shout, "Mister Webb, to the left!"

Webb saw two men riding to intercept them. He glanced back and saw a third, 300 yards farther away but closing in. To the right came another.

"Let's give them a race," he said. "Stretch 'em!"

He spurred hard, urging his horse to all the speed it had. Donovan's mount had a hard time keeping up, and the animal's reins grew taut on Webb's saddlehorn. Webb saw that Ellie was falling behind. She couldn't hold the pace. He slowed, hoping to give her a chance.

A movement ahead of him caught his eye. Two more riders, directly in their path. These men were waiting to head them off. Webb caught the glint of gunmetal in the sun. He heard a warning shot, fired into the air. He saw suddenly the futility of trying to outrun these men. He raised his hand as a signal and began to rein in his horse.

He was breathing hard as he brought the animal to a stop. Ellie and Johnny and Florentino gathered about him, their eyes asking him what they could do now.

Webb pointed ahead. "Look yonder. The river!"

He could see it now, or rather he could see the meandering line of brush that told him where the river would be. Its waters were hidden behind the green foliage. Not far now, probably not more than a mile. But it could as well have been twenty, for Donovan's men stood like a wall between them and the Rio Grande.

Johnny Willet asked, "We can't outrun them, and we can't count on outshootin' them with Ellie here, so what can we do?"

Webb frowned darkly as he watched the Donovan men warily begin closing in. An idea came to him.

"We're goin' to keep on ridin', Johnny. We're goin' to force our way through. Florentino, I'll swap you my pistol for your shotgun."

The Mexican handed Webb his weapon, taking Webb's in return. Webb turned to face Morg Donovan. "All right, Morg, you ride up here alongside of me. You're fixin' to be our ticket across that river." Morg hesitated. Webb tipped the gunmuzzle up, pointing it right into the man's eyes.

"Now," Webb said, "just calm and easy, let's move ahead, in a walk. Show them we're comin' through."

Seven Donovan men had lined up ahead of them, spreading themselves ten to fifteen feet apart. They stared in astonishment as the little posse started again, moving directly toward them. The outlaws had their guns ready but didn't try to use them. They just sat on their horses and stared.

Thirty feet from the widespread line, Webb lifted the shotgun barrel and placed the muzzle at the back of Morg Donovan's head.

"Spread apart there, boys," Webb said evenly to the men ahead of him. "We're comin' though."

Morg Donovan's eyes widened in fear, for there was a razor keenness to Webb's voice, and the shotgun was cold against Donovan's skin.

The Donovan men stared uncertainly, some bringing up their guns as if to use them, then thinking better of it. Slowly they spread apart and gave the posse room to pass.

Webb hoped his face didn't show the momentary relief that swept over him. He swallowed, resisting an urge to lick his dried lips. For the moment he had tipped the scales his own way. One bad move, one sign of weakness, and the whole bluff might fall in shambles. He held his breath and tried to avoid looking back.

He heard the horses then, and he knew they weren't being allowed to get away so easily. He glanced over his shoulder and saw what he had feared. The Donovan men had split. They were falling in to ride with the posse, half of them on one side, half on the other.

They trailed along watchfully, warily, like gaunt and hungry wolves stalking a little bunch of buffalo.

14

NEARER AND NEARER THEY CAME TO THE RIO GRANDE. IT would be at the river that the final decision must be made, that the bluff must be allowed to stand or be challenged in a blaze of fire and smoke.

To Webb it was no bluff. Though it cost his own life, he would squeeze this trigger, would kill Morg Donovan before he himself would die.

Webb's gaze searched eagerly ahead to the river and beyond. Sure, there was nothing to stop Donovan's men from following them across the river, to keep waiting for a chance to free Morg Donovan. But Webb doubted that they actually would. To him the river meant sanctuary. It was here that he must either win or lose. Across the Rio it wouldn't be far to help. He was sure that here at the river the Donovan crew would make its move or back away.

The Donovan men rode along abreast of Webb's group, four on one side, three on the other, keeping twenty or thirty feet from the posse. He could feel the eyes of the men watching him, waiting to seize upon any momentary advantage. Webb held the shotgun in a steady hand, the muzzle at Donovan's head.

This was the one chip he had left in the game.

Riding, he let his gaze move from one to another of the Donovan men, weighing them, judging them. His brother

Sandy was not among them. Florentino hadn't lied. Sandy wasn't with the Donovan gang, and Webb felt sure he never had been.

But Augie Brock was there. Augie Brock, who had been Sandy's friend. Beside Augie rode another youth of about Sandy's size and age. This, Webb reasoned, must have been the one with Augie in the bank holdup at Dry Fork, the one so many people had taken to be Sandy. Conscience chewed on Webb for having even considered the possibility that Sandy could have outlawed.

He saw nervous stress weighing on Augie Brock. Webb said, "Augie, you've got yourself in awful rough company."

The youth said, "Webb, you can boss Sandy around, but you ain't goin' to tell me nothin'."

"Wasn't tryin' to tell you anything, just want you to take a hard look and see for yourself. You don't really fit in with a bunch like that. Is this the best you had hoped for?"

Augie said, "This company suits me just fine." But his voice carried no real conviction. Webb thought he could sense misgiving.

They were nearer the river now. The ageless Rio Grande flowed ahead of them just 300 yards, then 200, then 100. The tension was winding tighter in Webb.

Thirty yards from the river one of the Donovan men—one Webb had taken as Donovan's *segundo*—suddenly spurred his horse up and circled in front of the group, stopping there. He placed himself squarely in Webb's path. "All right, mister lawman, I reckon we'll stop and parley a little."

"Parley about what?" Webb asked evenly. "We're crossin' that river, and Morg Donovan is goin' with us."

Webb didn't stop his horse. The man retreated a little, allowing Webb to move closer to the river. Then, abruptly, the rider seemed to make up his mind that this was as far as it went. He made a quick signal with his hand. The other six Donovan riders pushed in closer. Each held a gun. But then, so did Webb and Johnny and Florentino. With the shotgun pointed at Donovan's head, it looked like a standoff.

The leader declared, "We're callin' your bluff, lawman. We want Morg Donovan."

Webb's eyes narrowed. "Back off. We're takin' him across the river."

"You're forgettin', there's only four of you, and one is a woman. We could kill the whole bunch before you could wink an eye."

Webb said flatly, "But I'd see it comin' soon enough to pull this trigger. I don't aim to see Morg Donovan turned loose on the country again. Before I'd let that happen, I'd kill him like I'd kill a lobo wolf! Back off now or I'll give you Morg Donovan *dead!*"

The outlaw's face twisted in frustration. Looking into the angry eyes, Webb could almost see a dozen ideas flashing through the man's mind and being rejected as quickly as they came. Gradually the outlaw's mouth hardened. He flicked a glance at one of the other Donovan men, a Mexican.

"Juan, you're closest to the woman. Put that rifle of yours on her, the way the lawman has that shotgun on Morg."

Webb felt his blood chill. If there was a weakness in his own group, it was Ellie.

The outlaw said with a new confidence: "Now, lawman, you strike me as bein' a man with a conscience. Bad as you want Donovan, you wouldn't trade this lady for him, would you?" He answered his own question. "No, I reckon not. Now we got the same hand in this game as you have. You'd risk your own life, but not this woman's."

Morg Donovan gave a long sigh of relief and slumped a little. His tongue moved across dried lips. "Good work, Trace." He turned to face Webb. "Told you, didn't I, Matlock? The boys wouldn't let me down."

Webb touched the shotgun to Morg's neck. "Just you hold still, Morg. You're still my prisoner. I haven't turned you loose." Morg had started to grin, but the grin disappeared. Webb glanced toward the shaking Augie Brock. "Augie, you've eaten many a meal in Miss Ellie's place, and some of them when you couldn't afford to pay her."

Consternation came into Augie's eyes. "Miss Ellie, what did you have to come down here for, anyway?"

Ellid didn't answer. Her face was ashen, and Webb suspected she was too scared even to speak. Webb said, "Augie, she came because it was the right thing to do. Now you owe it to her to do the right thing yourself."

Augie looked as if he wanted to break down and cry. "You got no right to ask me. I didn't want nothin' like this to happen. I ain't goin' to take no hand in it, no hand at all."

Webb said, "If she dies, Augie, her blood will be on you."

The outlaw named Trace said, "Wrong, lawman. She's your responsibility. What you goin' to do?"

Ellie cried out, "Don't turn him loose, Webb. Not after all we've been through."

Webb looked at the Mexican. Trace said, "If you're wonderin' whether Juan will do it or not, don't bother yourself. Won't be the first woman he ever killed. Slit his own wife's throat because he caught her with another man. Juan ain't got no particular use for women. One looks about the same as another to him."

The held-in breath slowly went out of Webb, and he sagged. He had hoped for help from Augie Brock. From the hard look in the Mexican's eyes, Webb had no doubt the man would kill Ellie without batting an eyelash. Webb swallowed, the strength gone from him.

"You'll let her go if I turn Morg over to you?"

Trace said, "We'll talk about it."

Webb glanced at Morg Donovan. "How about it, Morg? Leave her alone?" He pushed a little on the shotgun to be sure Morg felt the cold rim of the muzzle against his neck.

"All right, I'll let her go."

Webb said bitterly, "To get this close and lose . . ." He grimaced and lowered the shotgun. He glanced at the man named Trace. "All right, Morg is yours."

"Drop that shotgun, then. And make your men drop their guns."

Webb glanced around. "Johnny, Florentino . . ." The two complied.

"Six-shooters too," said Trace. When that was done, the Mexican lowered the rifle he had held pointed at Ellie. Ellie sagged. Weakly she stepped to the ground and leaned against her horse, her hands over her eyes.

The color was drained from Morg's face as he pulled away

from Webb. He rode up to the man named Trace. "Here, cut me loose."

Trace took a knife and cut the rawhide that held Morg's hands to the saddle. Morg flexed his wrists and doubled and loosened his fists, rubbing to aid the circulation. Presently he looked back at Webb Matlock, his face clouded in hatred.

"Matlock, I owe you a debt. And if there's one thing the Donovans always do, it's pay their debts."

He held out his hand toward the nearest of his men. The man handed him a pistol. Morg swung the weapon toward Webb.

Ellie screamed, "No!" and leaped toward Morg. Morg's horse shied away at the sudden flare of skirts. Morg's hand flew upward, and his first shot missed.

In the moment of confusion, his own horse rearing, Webb quit the saddle. Morg tried with one hand to curb his mount and with the other to aim at the moving man. He missed a second time.

Ellie had turned back to where Webb had dropped the shotgun. She scooped it up from the hard ground. She cried, "Webb!" and pitched the gun to him. He caught it in both hands. Then, with no time to bring it to his shoulder and aim, he swung it against his hip, brought the muzzle up and squeezed the trigger.

The blast hit Morg Donovan full in the face and bowled him backward as if he had been struck by a sledge. Without a sound he slid off the horse and dropped lifeless to the ground. The shooting had thrown the horses into confusion and panic. The men struggled to bring them under control. Then they sat in their saddles and gazed horror-struck at the sight of Morg Donovan lying face down, the ground slowly reddening around him. The horses began to act up again, catching the smell of blood.

Trace said shakenly, "Just like Clabe. Just like Clabe." He turned to face Webb, who stood with the empty, smoking shotgun slack in his hand. "All promises are off, mister lawman. There ain't a one of you goin' back across that river now."

Augie Brock's voice broke through. "Let them alone, Trace!"

Trace looked around into the bore of Angie's pistol. "What the hell do you think you're doin', kid?"

"I'm stoppin' you. Spillin' their blood won't help Donavan now. Besides, I don't think you'll want to tangle with that bunch comin' yonder on the other side of the river. Look!"

The outlaw's head jerked to follow the sharp nod of Augie's chin. A whispered, "Damn!" escaped him.

Across the river, ten or a dozen men came pushing their horses hard.

Trace said, "We've flushed all the law there is in Texas. Let's get out of here!"

The outlaws swung their horses around and spurred south, forgetting about Morg Donovan, forgetting the little posse in the face of the larger one. All fled but Augie Brock. He held back, his head lowered in shame. He let his pistol slide into the holster. "Miss Ellie, I feel awful bad. I remember all the times you fed me when I was hungry. And there I was, about to back off and let them kill you."

Webb said, "Augie, you might have been slow, but you finally came around. We're much obliged."

Augie wasn't satisfied until he heard it from Ellie herself. "You did real fine, Augie," she said weakly. "And thank you."

Augie looked anxiously toward the river. The first of the riders already were splashing into the water from the other side.

Webb said, "Augie, the fact that you helped us will go a long ways with a jury. Run now and you'll run till the day you die."

Augie said, "I know, but I sure don't fancy none of them jails." He mounted his horse and started to run. He went perhaps 50 yards and pulled up. He turned and came back with his head down. He dismounted slowly. "You promise, Webb?"

Webb said, "I'll help you all I can."

Augie shrugged, accepting the inevitable. "I thought it'd

be a fancy life, ridin' with the wild bunch. Truth of it is, I was scared to death of most of them. And that *tequila*, it always made me kind of sick."

The riders reached the near bank and pulled their horses to a stop. Webb looked up gratefully into familiar faces— tall old Quince Pyburn with some of Jess Leggett's cowboys. And there was Sandy Matlock! Webb's mouth fell open in surprise. The sun struck and flashed against something metal on Sandy's shirt. It was a Texas Ranger badge.

Sandy jumped to the ground and rushed to his brother's side. "Webb, you all right?" He glanced then at Ellie Donovan, who still knelt where she had grabbed up the shotgun. "You, Miss Ellie? How about you?"

She nodded and tried to smile and began to cry softly instead. Webb took her hands, lifting her to her feet. He put his arms around her and held her close against him.

"She's all right, Sandy. We're all goin' to be just fine."

Quince Pyburn dropped stiffly to one knee to look at the outlaw's body. "Clabe Donovan," he said quietly. "Looks like we got to bury him again."

"It's not Clabe," Webb told him. "It's Morg." As briefly as he could, he told of Morg's masquerade, and the reasons for it.

A tall man strode up, a stranger to Webb. "Webb Matlock?" he asked. Webb saw that this man wore a Ranger's badge like Sandy's. The Ranger said, "I'm Russ Talley. Been hearin' a right smart about you from Sandy."

Webb frowned in puzzlement. "I don't understand, Talley. How did all of you happen to be here?"

"Judge Upshaw sent for the Rangers before he . . . before he died. Captain detailed me, and because Sandy knew the country, he sent him along to show me the way. Mister Pyburn there, he told us where you'd gone. We gathered a bunch of volunteers and came to help. We couldn't cross over the way you did, but we scattered up and down the river to be around in case you needed help when you came back. We heard shooting a while ago and came running."

That, Webb remembered, would have been the signal given by the first Donovan man who spotted them.

Looking now, he could see still other riders coming, drawn by the sound of the guns. No telling how many miles of river they had patrolled.

Talley said, "Matlock, that brother of yours is going to make a good Ranger. A little green yet, and rough in spots, but he has the makings. You should be proud of him."

Webb said soberly, "I am."

Sandy had walked over to his friend, Augie Brock. He stood with one hand on the worried youth's shoulder, talking in a voice too quiet for Webb to hear the words. Webb thought he knew the gist of Sandy's conversation, though: that Sandy would stick by Augie and help him all he could.

Presently Sandy came back to Webb, his hands shoved deep into his pockets, his head down. "Webb, I'm sorry if I caused you any worry. I left here mad. Aimed to make myself into a full-fledged Ranger before I came back. Wanted to show you what I could do. Now I can see that I ought to've written you and Birdie a letter." He frowned. "You should've seen the hot reception they gave me in Dry Fork. I hadn't no more than got off my horse till a dozen people was holdin' guns on me. Lieutenant Talley, he had to do a lot of explainin' before they'd turn me loose."

Indignation flared in Sandy's face. "Did you know, Webb, there was folks in town actually thought I'd outlawed? Thought I'd gone off and joined up with Donovan's bunch? Can you imagine anybody gettin' a crazy notion like that?"

Webb turned away to keep Sandy from seeing the sheepish look in his eyes. "It's hard to imagine."

Some of the men had rolled Morg Donovan's body in a blanket and were tying it across a horse. Lieutenant Talley watched the job finished, then said, "We better get back across the river. We've got no real right to be here."

Webb leaned down and took Ellie's hands. "Feel like ridin' again? We can stop on the other side somewhere, and you can get all the rest you need."

She nodded. "I want to put this place behind me." She started to get up but paused a moment. "Webb, now that it's over, I'm almost glad it turned out this way, that it wasn't Clabe."

Webb said, "Ellie, maybe you ought to take a long trip someplace, like San Antonio or one of those other big towns. Do somethin' different a while, put your mind on other things. You'll be surprised how fast you'll forget all this."

She arose, her face turned up toward his. "That sounds like a good idea, Webb, but I don't want to go alone. Will you take me?"

Webb gripped her hands tighter. "I'll take you, Ellie. Anywhere you want to go."

Look for

LONE STAR RISING:

The Texas Rangers Trilogy
(0-765-30891-6)

by **ELMER KELTON**

Now available
from Forge Books